"W
all ı

Dale scowled at him, not happy at the rapid-fire questions. "Please stand back, sir," he said firmly, trying to bar the man from getting any closer. He couldn't help but notice the man had dark wavy hair, cheekbones to kill for, and big baby blue eyes.

"Mrs. Wilson works for me. Is she all right?" the man demanded.

"The paramedics are checking her over now," Dale said.

"How did the fire start?" His tone suggested he expected Dale to answer all his questions right then.

Dale took a deep breath to stop the angry response on the tip of his tongue. "Sir, get back behind the cordon, please. We'll be able to answer your questions later. Let me get back to doing my job."

"Don't you know who I am?"

Dale's fraying patience snapped. "I don't care if you're Lord Muckety-Muck himself, *sir*. Get back behind the cordon *now*!"

"Who the hell do you think you're talking to?" the man growled.

"I'm talking to the man who's stopping me doing my job."

Welcome to
Dreamspun Desires

Dear Reader,

Love is the dream. It dazzles us, makes us stronger, and brings us to our knees. Dreamspun Desires tell stories of love featuring your favorite heartwarming heroes, captivating plots, and exotic locations. Stories that make your breath catch and your imagination soar.

In the pages of these wonderful love stories, readers can escape to a world where love conquers all, the tenderness of a first kiss sweeps you away, and your heart pounds at the sight of the one you love.

When you put it all together, you find romance in its truest form.

Love always finds a way.

Elizabeth North

Executive Director
Dreamspinner Press

Sue Brown

THE FIREMAN'S POLE

DREAMSPUN DESIRES

PUBLISHED BY

DREAMSPINNER
PRESS

Published by
DREAMSPINNER PRESS

5032 Capital Circle SW, Suite 2, PMB# 279,
Tallahassee, FL 32305-7886 USA
www.dreamspinnerpress.com

This is a work of fiction. Names, characters, places, and incidents either are the product of author imagination or are used fictitiously, and any resemblance to actual persons, living or dead, business establishments, events, or locales is entirely coincidental.

The Fireman's Pole
© 2017 Sue Brown.

Cover Art
© 2017 Bree Archer.
http://www.breearcher.com
Cover content is for illustrative purposes only and any person depicted on the cover is a model.

All rights reserved. This book is licensed to the original purchaser only. Duplication or distribution via any means is illegal and a violation of international copyright law, subject to criminal prosecution and upon conviction, fines, and/or imprisonment. Any eBook format cannot be legally loaned or given to others. No part of this book may be reproduced or transmitted in any form or by any means, electronic or mechanical, including photocopying, recording, or by any information storage and retrieval system, without the written permission of the Publisher, except where permitted by law. To request permission and all other inquiries, contact Dreamspinner Press, 5032 Capital Circle SW, Suite 2, PMB# 279, Tallahassee, FL 32305-7886, USA, or www.dreamspinnerpress.com.

ISBN: 978-1-63533-654-2
Digital ISBN: 978-1-63533-655-9
Library of Congress Control Number: 2017938685
Published October 2017
v. 1.1

Printed in the United States of America

This paper meets the requirements of
ANSI/NISO Z39.48-1992 (Permanence of Paper).

SUE BROWN is owned by her dogs and two children. When she isn't following their orders, she can be found with her laptop in Starbucks, drinking latte and eating chocolate.

Sue discovered M/M romance at the time she woke up to find two men kissing on her favorite television series. The kissing was hot and tender and Sue wanted to write about these men. She may be late to the party, but she's made up for it since, writing fan fiction until she was brave enough to venture out into the world of original fiction.

Sue can be found at:
Website: www.suebrownstories.com
Blog: suebrownsstories.blogspot.co.uk
Twitter: @suebrownstories
Facebook: www.facebook.com/suebrownstories

Chapter One

7:15.

"Oh no. Oh no, no, no!" Dale sat up in bed, blinking away sleep as he stared in horror at the time on his phone. "I set the bloody alarm. I know I did!"

7:16.

No matter how much he scowled at the screen, the time didn't reverse. He must have forgotten to set his alarm clock the previous night, and far from having a leisurely start to the day before leaving for Calminster Fire Station, he had less than forty minutes to get ready, eat breakfast, and arrive at his new job.

7:17.

Throwing himself out of bed, Dale swore loudly and profusely at his phone, himself, and the world as he rushed down the stairs to the bathroom, to shower, shave, and dress.

Dale gave up on the idea of breakfast and, grabbing his keys and wallet, headed out of the tiny cottage he had rented. His transfer had come through much quicker than he'd expected, and he hadn't had time to find a place of his own before starting at his new station. His new commander had organized temporary accommodation. His cottage, like most of the village, was part of the Calminster estate. Dale hadn't been to see Calminster Hall yet, but he'd been told it was worth a visit.

He wasn't thinking about stately homes as he backed his red Mini down the narrow lane as fast as he could and out onto the main road. Fortunately, the fire station was on the outskirts of the small village of Calminster, and Dale didn't have far to drive. He'd run past the fire station the previous day and could easily have walked if he hadn't been stupid enough to oversleep.

Driving his Mini faster than he should have done through the narrow streets, Dale incurred the wrath of a little old lady who'd been about to step out into the road. He took a deep breath, waved his hand apologetically, and tried to ignore the fact she used a very expressive gesture in return.

"Slow down, Maloney," he muttered. "You're not going to endear yourself to the local inhabitants if you take out one of the wrinklies on your first day."

Dale slowed down considerably, but he managed to arrive at the fire station with five minutes to spare. As he parked, two other cars pulled in beside him. The men got out and studied him speculatively.

"You must be the new bloke," one of them said. From his sparse gray hair shaved back to a stubble and laughter lines around his eyes, Dale hazarded a guess he was nearing retirement.

Dale held out his hand. "Dale Maloney."

"Mick Smith, and he's Keith Richards. No, not that Keith Richards—it really pisses him off if you make that joke to his face." Mick had a bright smile and a firm handshake for the new guy.

Dale decided it was simpler just to shake Keith's hand. "Hi, good to meet you."

Keith, who seemed about the same age as Dale, smiled at him and said, "Ignore Smith. The rest of us do. He's like a mother hen."

"Thanks," Mick said dryly and shoved Keith by the shoulder.

They scuffled for a minute or two while Dale waited for them to calm down. Eventually they separated and showed him into the fire station. Mick introduced him to the station commander and the watch commander, then disappeared, muttering about coffee.

TANK Wembley, the watch commander, was a huge big-chested man with a ready smile and enormous hands. Dale had a thing about hands, men's hands specifically, and it was something he always noticed. He didn't like men with small hands.

"Morning, Maloney. It's Dale, isn't it?"

"Yes, sir."

Tank laughed. "Call me Tank. No one stands to attention here."

"Especially Tank," the station commander said with a wry smile. "Lee Fang. Call me Sir."

"Yes, sir."

Tank laughed and clapped Dale across the back, only Dale's excellent reflexes preventing him from flying across the room. "You'll get used to us soon enough."

Dale pasted on a smile and hoped it was true. Despite the military way his previous station had been run, Dale had liked his job on the outskirts of Nottingham. The only reason he'd chosen to leave and move halfway across the country was because of his lying, cheating scum of an ex-partner.

The fallout from his breakup had been messy, and the worst thing was none of his colleagues had a clue Dale was hurting. He'd come home early to propose to his boyfriend and discovered Baz in bed with one of the female crew. He'd walked out, his fingers clutched around the ring box in his pocket. Neither he nor Baz had officially come out at work, and the following day he'd had to watch Susan and Baz hold hands and declare they'd moved in together to congratulations from everyone at the station. Susan had apologized to Dale for "upsetting their friendship," but it wasn't her fault. She'd had no clue Baz was even in a relationship with Dale. Her apology was the moment Dale knew he'd have to move. He couldn't stay at the station and watch Baz romance Susan. On the sly Baz had still been trying to convince Dale that even if he stayed in a relationship with Susan, everything could stay the same between them. Dale had stared at Susan for a long moment before he walked into the station commander's office and handed in his resignation. He told Baz to collect his gear, rented out his house, and used his leave to finish at the station as soon as he could. Then he applied for the next available transfer anywhere in the country.

Which was why he ended up in Calminster, one hundred and sixty-five miles away from Baz, and he was just about to find out if he was going to have a problem with—

"I'm gay," Dale said abruptly.

The two men stared at him.

He stared back and waited. Eventually Tank broke the awkward silence.

"You expecting us to do something? Throw a party? Wave a rainbow flag? Find a unicorn?"

"I want to know if I'm going to have a problem." Dale didn't want to sound defiant on his first day, but he wasn't going back into another closet to pacify their feelings.

Lee Fang shook his head. "Not with me, Maloney. Tank's just an arsehole. If you have any trouble, just let me, Tank, or Mick know."

Dale nodded. "I can hold my own, but I won't take shit from anyone." He'd been stoic and in the closet, and look where that had got him. Dale refused to do that again, even if he had to make his point with his fists.

"And I don't expect you to," Lee said.

"You tell me if they do," Tank agreed. "I *am* an arsehole, but I don't allow issues with anyone. We've got a damned good crew here and a couple of women who'll bend you in half if you give them shit." Tank cocked his head. "You're not likely to do that, are you?"

"I have no problem with women firefighters," Dale confirmed.

As long as they didn't fuck his boyfriend.

DALE followed Tank to the rec room to meet the rest of White watch. He felt like a tiny tug boat swept along in the wake of his new watch commander. Eight pairs of eyes, including a woman who was uncomfortably similar to Susan, stared at him as he walked in the room.

"This is Dale Maloney," Tank said. "He's gay. Give him shit and I'll write you up on a charge."

Dale choked. "What the hell?"

Tank raised an eyebrow. "You wanted them to know, didn't you?"

"Well, yeah, but I thought I was going to tell them."

The older man he'd met earlier laughed and beckoned him over. Dale had forgotten his name. "Here, grab a coffee. Tank's got the social graces of a pig. We don't care what you are as long as you don't eat the last doughnut."

"Who gets to eat the last doughnut?"

"Mick," everyone in the room chorused in unison and Mick took a bow.

"I'll remember that." Dale winked at him.

Mick winked back, handed Dale a mug and a doughnut, and then stuffed the last doughnut from the plate into his mouth.

"Gross." Tank pulled a face.

Dale sank into a chair and focused on drinking his tea. He hadn't expected Tank just to announce he was gay like that. Everyone was so laid-back about the announcement. None of them had batted an eyelid. Dale refused to step back into the closet, but he'd been prepared for a fight. It was almost anticlimactic.

The woman leaned over. "I'm Emma."

"Dale." He was big enough not to judge her for being an identikit version of the woman who stole his boyfriend.

"Ignore them." She jerked her thumb at Tank and Mick who bickered amiably, among sprays of crumbs. "They're always the same."

"Maloney."

Dale turned to Mick.

"You going to eat that doughnut?"

Dale stuffed the whole thing in his mouth before Mick could swipe it from him. He chewed to the sound of Emma's peel of laughter and Mick's disappointed groan.

"You're going to drive Bertha today," Tank said.

"Bertha?"

"She's the big old bus out there. All the appliances have names."

Dale didn't have a problem with that. Old Bertha was a Scania, an appliance he was familiar with driving.

Calminster Fire Station was a total anomaly for a rural area. Because of its proximity to a city, Calminster was manned twenty-four hours instead of part-time. The station commander had been honest with Dale when he interviewed for the job, saying he didn't know how long the situation would last, but Dale had been desperate to get away from Baz, and he decided to take the chance as he had income from the rent on his old house if he had to find another job.

"The village has a May Day parade in a few weeks, and big Bertha is one of the attractions," Tank said. "We've just got to go down to the village green today and meet with Lord Calminster. He's the organizer of the parade."

Dale stared at him skeptically. "Lord Calminster? Seriously, a lord?"

"Oh yeah, we have a real live lord of the manor. We all bow and scrape to him and tug our forelocks."

"What the hell is a forelock?"

"No idea," Tank confessed. "Just mind your p's and q's around him."

Dale had never met a lord before, and he wasn't sure he wanted to meet one now if he was expected to slime all over some nob. Still, he knew the village was dependent on Calminster Hall for much of its income, and Dale was living in a house owned by the estate. He supposed he had to toe the party line and bow and scrape when he met Lord Calminster. "When are we going?"

Tank glanced at the clock. "We may as well go now. Then we can be back in time for lunch. Mick, can you give the Hall a call to let them know we're on our way?"

"Sure," Mick said before he downed the rest of his coffee.

Tank took Dale over to meet Bertha. "Bertha was named after the previous station commander's mother."

"Is this one named after Fang's mother?" Dale pointed to the nearest, shiniest, definitely new appliance.

Tank's lips twitched. "He refused to have an appliance named after her. He and his mother don't have the best of relationships. We had a competition to name her. The boys wanted something in keeping with Fang."

Dale wandered around the appliance and found the name. "Buffy? You called her Buffy?"

"It's better than Bella," Tank said, a shade defensively.

"Who's Bella?" Dale furrowed his brow.

"*Twilight*?"

Dale shook his head, and Tank rolled his eyes.

"I can tell you don't have a girlfriend or a daughter."

The shrill sound of the alarm drowned whatever else Tank was going to say. Mick emerged with details of the callout. "Shit! It's Mrs. Wilson's house. We've got to move."

Tank and Dale headed for Bertha, Keith and Mick hard on their heels.

"Who's Mrs. Wilson?" Dale said.

"She works up at the Hall," Tank said. "She's lived in the village all her life."

"I'll drive," Mick said. "You can take Bertha out next time."

Dale could see the smoke as soon as they pulled out of the station. By the time they arrived at the narrow cul-de-sac, Dale could see a crowd of people blocking the road. Mick sounded the siren to get them out of the way and carefully inched down between the cars to maneuver near the cottage.

As they jumped down and started unrolling the hoses, Tank went to talk to the neighbors. He came back, a worried expression on his face. "The neighbors don't know where Mrs. Wilson is. She didn't respond to them banging on the door, and they phoned the Hall. She's not there either."

Mick looked at the cottage and paled. "If she was in there, she's a goner." The downstairs was consumed by flames, and the upstairs level was full of black smoke.

Dale had been a fireman for long enough to see plenty of people trapped by fire, but it never got any easier, no matter how many callouts he attended.

"Keith and Dale, go around the back and see if you can find her," Tank ordered. "Mick, we've got to get these idiots out of the way."

The side gate was securely locked, and Dale had to kick it a couple of times before the wood around the lock splintered. He shoved the gate open, Keith following hard on his heels down the narrow side passage. Benches full of pots of herbs and flowers made negotiating the passageway more difficult, but Dale didn't have time to right the pots he knocked over. He couldn't see Mrs. Wilson in the small cottage garden, and his heart sank. Flames had consumed the kitchen, and if she hadn't got out, he held out little hope of her survival. Then Dale saw something pink behind the low wall that separated the patio and the lawn.

"Over here," he yelled at Keith.

They rushed over, and to Dale's immense relief, they found an elderly lady lying crumpled behind the wall. She was unconscious and had a huge bruise on the right side of her face. She was alive but cold, and her pulse was slow. As Dale examined her, she moaned, and he contemplated leaving her there and getting paramedics to check her out *in situ*. But then the kitchen windows blew out, shattering glass over them. Dale and Keith tried to shelter the unconscious woman as best they could.

"We've got to move her," Keith said over the roar of the flames.

Dale gathered Mrs. Wilson into his arms. She was tiny and no problem for him to carry. They retreated back down the side path, plant pots scattering in their wake. Paramedics rushed forward with a gurney and Dale laid her down gently.

"She's alive but very cold, and her pulse is thready. Be careful of glass. The windows blew out."

The paramedics nodded and wheeled her to the ambulance.

Dale turned to go to Tank for his orders, but his way was barred by a young guy ducking the cordon and rushing toward the ambulance. "Get back, sir." The man tried to push past him, but Dale blocked his path.

"What's happened? Is Mrs. Wilson all right?"

Dale scowled at him, not happy at the rapid-fire questions. "Please stand back, sir," he said firmly, trying to bar the man from getting any closer. He couldn't help but notice the man had dark wavy hair, cheekbones to kill for, and big baby blue eyes.

"Mrs. Wilson works for me. Is she all right?" the man demanded.

"The paramedics are checking her over now," Dale said.

"How did the fire start?" His tone suggested he expected Dale to answer all his questions right then.

Dale took a deep breath to stop the angry response on the tip of his tongue. "Sir, get back behind the cordon, please. We'll be able to answer your questions later. Let me get back to doing my job."

"Don't you know who I am?"

Dale's fraying patience snapped. "I don't care if you're Lord Muckety-Muck himself, *sir*. Get back behind the cordon *now!*"

"Who the hell do you think you're talking to?" the man growled.

"I'm talking to the man who's stopping me doing my job."

"I'm her landlord."

"Then you can wait until the fire is out and we'll see if this is your fault," Dale snapped.

"What do you mean?"

"These are old cottages. Who knows when the electrics were updated?"

"The electrics were replaced in all the cottages in the road last year," the man retorted, "and I don't appreciate your implication."

Tank joined them. "Maloney, what's going on here? Your lordship?"

Your lordship? This was Lord Calminster? Dale was expecting someone middle-aged and balding with a paunch. He should be wearing a tweed jacket with patches on the elbows, not a killer suit, and where was his cap? Oh God, he really had just insulted Lord Muckety-Muck. He'd be clapped up in the village stocks before he said another word.

"You said you were her landlord."

"He owns the whole village," Tank said.

Of course he does.

Lord Calminster ignored Dale, directing his question at Tank. "What's happened? Is Mrs. Wilson all right?"

"She was lucky," Tank said. "Maloney found her in the garden. Another few minutes and she might not have been so lucky. I can't say the same for the cottage."

At the end of Tank's brief summary, Lord Calminster deigned to notice Dale's existence. "Thank you for rescuing Mrs. Wilson."

Dale curled his lip at his grudging thanks. "You're welcome." He stalked off to help the others, leaving Tank to deal with the arrogant SOB.

Emma glanced over as he took his place on the hose. "His lordship got here quickly."

"Yeah," Dale grunted.

"Arrogant bastard, isn't he?"

Dale gave her a brief smile. "So it isn't just me?"

She laughed. "It's not just you."

As they finally rolled away the hoses, Tank joined them. "What was that all about?"

"What do you mean?" Dale asked.

"You and his lordship." Tank raised an eyebrow. "I thought you were going to punch each other's lights out."

"I might have… um… accused him of being a negligent landlord."

Tank snorted out a laugh. "You remember he's your landlord too?"

"You mean I've upset the wrong person?"

"And on your first day. Way to go." Tank clapped Dale on the back, nearly driving him to his knees. Dale gritted his teeth as he recovered his balance. The watch commander obviously didn't know his own strength.

"Is he going to throw me out on the streets?" Dale asked. "Am I going to have to find a park bench to sleep on? Does Calminster have a park?"

Tank grinned wickedly. "'Round the back of the church. The land was donated by his lordship's father."

"Shit, my mother's going to kill me," Dale muttered.

"Your mother?" Tank furrowed his brow, obviously confused, as he helped Dale stow the last hose.

"She loved *Downton Abbey*. Oh well, it can only get better from here."

"If you say so."

Dale noticed Tank didn't sound convinced. He wasn't sure he'd convinced himself. But it was too late now. He'd have to make nice with the lord of the manor another day.

Chapter Two

"DON'T you know who I am?"

The second the words passed Benedict Raleigh's lips, he knew he'd made a mistake as the fire officer's expression darkened.

"I don't care if you're Lord Muckety-Muck himself, *sir*. Get back behind the cordon *now*!"

Benedict Raleigh, nineteenth Baron Calminster of Calminster Hall, had no idea who the new firefighter was, but he needed to get the hell out of Ben's way. Mrs. Wilson was the closest thing Ben had to a family, and nobody was going to stop him seeing how she was.

When Colson, his butler, had burst into his study and told Ben about the fire, Ben had grabbed his shoes, told his three dogs to stay, and run as fast as he could through the formal gardens to the village green, Colson close behind him. He didn't dare tell Colson to stay behind. Colson and Mrs. Wilson were family, especially since Ben's parents had died.

Now he was being blocked by an outsider with an attitude, and even if the guy did fulfill every fireman fantasy Ben had ever had, the man needed to understand who exactly he was dealing with. He was at the point of throwing his *Lord Muckety-Muck* title in Maloney's face when Tank came over. Ben tried to hold back the smirk when Maloney realized Ben was the lord of the manor, but from the expression on Maloney's face, he wasn't entirely successful.

Ben was relieved to discover from Tank that Mrs. Wilson was alive, and then one of the paramedics beckoned him over. Ben recognized her as someone who lived in the village. He jogged over to the gurney where Colson was talking to Mrs. Wilson.

"Mrs. Wilson has minor burns, mild hypothermia, and probably a concussion, your lordship," the paramedic said. "She's conscious now. We'll take her to hospital."

Mrs. Wilson grabbed his hand as he leant over the gurney, confusion on her face. "Mr. Ben. What are you doing here? Who are these people?"

"Good to see you awake, Mrs. Wilson," Ben said, trying not to show how distressed he was. "You had a bit of a fall."

"I did?" She wrinkled her face, trying to remember. "I was making my breakfast. I tripped over Sparkles. I don't remember anything else. Mr. Ben, could you check I switched off the grill? I'm making toast."

Ben flicked a glance at the paramedic and Colson, who shook their heads. Evidently she didn't know anything about the fire. He decided that could wait until later. "I'll phone your daughter. She can meet you at the hospital."

"Don't bother Sandra. She's busy and I'm all right," she said hoarsely. "I just need a sit down and a cup of tea."

"You know Sandra will have my guts if I don't ring her," Ben said.

"We need to go." The paramedic tried to move the gurney but Mrs. Wilson gasped and held on to Ben's hand.

"What about Sparkles? Is she all right?"

Sparkles was a mean-spirited cat who was the center of Mrs. Wilson's life. Dogs in the neighborhood would flee at the sight of Sparkles on the prowl.

"I promise I'll find her," Ben said. "Let's get you to hospital."

"I'll go with Mrs. Wilson to the hospital," Colson said. "I'll call you if there's any news."

Ben gently squeezed her hand. "I'll see you there, Mrs. Wilson. Don't run away."

She gave a weak laugh, which turned into a hacking cough, and the paramedics frowned, shuffling Ben out of the way so they could assess her.

Reluctantly, Ben stepped back to let the paramedics get her into the ambulance; Colson climbed in with her. The blue lights flashed and onlookers scattered as the ambulance eased its way out of the cul-de-sac.

As Ben watched them go, a woman shoved a mug of coffee in his hands. He finished the drink although it tasted of ashes and smoke, because he was aware of her eyes upon him, and knew he would just get another one thrust in his hand if he didn't.

Finally, the firemen rolled away the hoses and prepared to leave, including Maloney. Ben studied him. He was tall and broad-shouldered, and even covered in soot, he was stunning. Their eyes locked for a moment, and Ben flushed at being caught staring. Then one of the other firefighters slapped Maloney on the shoulder and

The Fireman's Pole

distracted him before he climbed into the Scania. Ben was aware of Maloney's final glance in his direction before the door shut with a clunk.

After the fire appliances had backed out of the cul-de-sac, the woman who'd given him the coffee approached him again. "Do you need anything, Lord Calminster?"

"I need to call Mrs. Wilson's daughter," Ben said. "I've got the number back at the Hall."

"I've got it on my phone. Do you want me to call?"

"I should do it," Ben said. "Could you send it to me?" He gave his number, and a minute later his phone vibrated. "I'll call Sandra now. Could you arrange to get clothes and things for Mrs. Wilson? She's got nothing left."

"The Women's Institute has begun a collection for her. We'll bring what we've collected over tonight, and the Ladies Group at the church is doing the same."

The ladies' groups in the village were a formidable bunch of women, and Ben had no doubt Mrs. Wilson would be provided for. Then Ben remembered Mrs. Wilson's concern for her cat.

"Mrs. Wilson is worried about Sparkles."

"I'll find her and take her in. She won't have gone far."

"Thank you." Ben smiled at her, a little embarrassed at not knowing who she was.

"I'm just glad they found her." The woman stuck her hand out. "I'm Lucie Jones."

"Benedict Raleigh."

Lucie's lips twitched. "I know."

Ben decided to escape before he said anything else stupid. He moved out of earshot of everyone else and called Mrs. Wilson's daughter.

"Hello?"

"Hi, is that Sandra?"

"Yes, it is." She sounded wary now. "I'm not buying anything."

"Sandra, it's Ben Raleigh."

"Mr. Ben, I mean, Lord Calminster. Is everything all right?"

"Yes. No. There's no easy way to break this news. There's been a fire, and your mum—"

"Oh my God! Mum…." Sandra sounded as if she was about to faint.

"She's okay, Sandra. I promise, she's alive. We found her in the garden. The paramedics have taken her to hospital, but she's all right. She's got mild hypothermia and a concussion."

"She's alive?" Sandra asked as if that was the only thing she could focus on.

"I promise. The paramedics wanted to check her over at the hospital. You can meet her there."

"I'll go now." Ben heard her moving around as she talked.

"I know this isn't important now, but I'll arrange a suite of rooms for her at the Hall when she's released, and neighbors are organizing clothes and necessities."

"Is it that bad? Can't she go back home?"

"I'm so sorry, Sandra, but the cottage needs extensive repairs."

"God!" Sandra went quiet for a while, and Ben could hear her swallowing as if she was trying not to cry. "I'll go to the hospital now."

Ben swallowed back the lump in his throat. "Colson is already there."

Sandra barked a short laugh. "Mum will tell me to go home as soon as I arrive. You know what she's like."

Now Ben laughed, conscious of a few shocked glances his way. "I know she won't want to stay in hospital for long. You can reassure her I'll get the estate manager to organize a new cottage in the next couple of days. I know she likes being in the village."

"You know her well."

"She's family," Ben said simply. "I've just got to sort things out here and I'll drive over to the hospital. I'll see you there."

Ben visited Mrs. Wilson's neighbors either side of her to check their homes weren't badly damaged. They were lucky; the solid stone walls had contained the blaze. He assured them the estate manager would be around later to talk to them about repairs before he walked slowly back to the Hall.

Calminster Hall was a large Georgian home nestling in the Hampshire countryside. To Benedict, it was home. He had lived in the house his entire life, and at twenty-three years old, he became Lord Calminster, nineteenth Baron of Calminster Hall, on the death of his father, a minor peer but extremely wealthy and an astute businessman. He'd started working for his father as a teenager, and his suggestions had helped to expand the businesses running on the estate. Fifteen years on, the Calminster Hall estate was a rare beast—a profitable country home.

As he reached the herb garden, his phone buzzed. Ben dug it out to see a message from his girlfriend.

We need to talk.

Ben rolled his eyes. The message was so typical of Sabrina. He quickly typed a message in return.

Later. Dealing with emergency.

His phone buzzed again, but he ignored it. Sabrina could wait. He needed to make sure Mrs. Wilson was okay before he worried about his girlfriend. The study doors were closed, so he walked around to what used to be the servants' door and entered the house. The dogs rushed to greet him, and Ben knelt to rub their ears and bellies. Frankie, the little Yorkshire terrier, sniffed at him curiously. Ben wrinkled his nose at the waft of soot and ash on his clothes and skin. He desperately needed a shower and a long drink of something cold to wash away the rank taste in his mouth.

Lisa glanced up from the pile of potatoes she was peeling when Ben walked into the kitchen in search of the drink. "We'll put Mrs. Wilson in the Rose Room, Lord Calminster, because of the lift. You know she struggles with the stairs. The room is being aired out now."

Ben pulled a jug of Mrs. Wilson's fresh lemonade out of the fridge. "You know she's going to complain at being in the master bedroom." He poured a glass and drank deeply, gasping at the sour taste, but it was exactly what he needed.

"I know, but it's the only one we have that's suitable. Do you want me to sort something else out instead?"

"It's fine with me, Lisa," Ben reassured him. "I need to talk to Barry about another cottage when she's ready."

"He's already checking into it. There's one down Primrose Lane that's been vacant for a while. And he's going to check on Mrs. Wilson's neighbors in case they need repairs."

Ben was unsurprised that his staff were several steps ahead of him. That's what he paid them for.

"I'll fill in a few shifts while she's in hospital, and we can sort out the others," Lisa said. "Go and rest for a moment. I'll bring you tea."

Ben rubbed his eyes. "I have to get to the hospital."

"Mr. Colson phoned me about five minutes ago. She's still waiting in A&E. You've got time for tea," she said firmly.

As Ben retreated to his personal study, he thought a little ruefully that his staff managed him, rather than him managing them. He needed a few moments to recover. His heart was still pounding at the fear that Mrs. Wilson had been killed in the blaze. She treated him like a grandson, and as far as Ben was concerned, she was the closest thing to family he had left, along with Colson. He slumped onto the sofa and closed his eyes, appreciating the comfort of the dogs snuggling around him. He would need to have a shower before he went to Accident and Emergency, or Mrs. Wilson would scold him. Ben rubbed his eyes and wished he hadn't, as they felt like sandpaper.

The tea arrived so quickly Ben suspected it had been ready and waiting for him. He smiled as Lisa brought in the tray of tea and sandwiches. "Thanks, Lisa."

"You're welcome, Mr. Ben. I have to remind you of something. What was it?" Lisa wrinkled her brow, then snapped her fingers. "Miss Sabrina just called. She's coming over tonight."

"She is?" Ben was damn sure they hadn't made plans, and she hadn't mentioned it in her texts. "Okay, thanks for the warning."

Once Lisa had departed, Ben growled under his breath. The last thing he wanted was Sabrina around tonight. It was going to be traumatic enough without her being there. He dug out his phone and tapped Sabrina's number.

"Hello, stranger."

Ben heard the edge in her silky tone and gritted his teeth.

"Sabrina, what's this about coming over?"

"I told you we need to talk."

"Sabrina, it's been a long day. We had a fire in the village. Mrs. Wilson's cottage is destroyed. Can't it wait?" Ben was hard put to keep the growl out of his voice.

"Who is Mrs. Wilson?"

Ben bit back his angry retort. It was a source of contention that Sabrina had never made the effort to get to know his staff. "She's my cook. You've met her several times."

"Oh. Is she all right?" Sabrina didn't sound as if she cared much about Mrs. Wilson.

"She's gone to A&E. I'm just about to go there."

"I suppose it can wait another day."

Now she sounded sulky, and Ben was tempted to end the call. He made an effort to gentle his tone. "I've got to go. I'll call you tomorrow. Goodbye."

He disconnected before she could say anything else and threw the phone onto the sofa. He wouldn't put it past her to turn up anyway. Ben growled as he picked up his tea. He shivered as he thought about what could've happened, and then, for some reason, that fireman popped into his mind. What was his name? Martin? Markus? Maloney. That was it. He pushed all Ben's buttons, even if he was an arrogant sod. Ben shook his head to clear his mind. He couldn't afford to be distracted by anyone, hot or otherwise.

Chapter Three

DESPITE Dale's run-in with the lord of the manor, he was settling in to his new home without any problems. From the moment he stepped into the Shepherd's Crook pub and a total stranger bought him a drink, he realized that rescuing Mrs. Wilson had got him into the village's good books quicker than anything else could.

His job was going well too. He still missed his old station, but the new crew were fun to work with, and there was enough work to keep him occupied. He tried not to think about Baz, but when he was on his own, it was hard not to feel acutely alone without someone to snuggle up to.

"We've got to do that fire inspection at the green today," Tank said in Dale's second week. "It's a formality because nothing changes from year to year, but gotta tick the boxes."

"You can drive, Maloney," Mick said. "It's about time you pulled your weight."

Dale flipped him off and got into the cab to familiarize himself with big Bertha. The other fire officers piled in, and Bertha got underway. Dale drove much slower than Mick, and Tank grumbled at the speed he was driving, but when Dale explained about nearly taking out an old lady on his first day, Tank howled with laughter.

"I bet that was Ava," Tank said. "You'd better hope she doesn't remember you, or you'll never be allowed to forget it."

"She was—very expressive," Dale said diplomatically.

"Definitely Ava," Mick said. "I learned all my swear words as a kid from her."

"I guess she had justification. I did nearly flatten her with my car."

"Just be careful around these lanes. Nobody goes slowly, and you'd be amazed how many times we get called out to cut people out of cars." Tank's usually cheery expression sobered rapidly. "The kids around here are always flipping their cars into the fields."

Dale wondered if Tank had lost someone in a car accident, but it was none of his business. Anyway, he had to concentrate on finding somewhere to park near the green. There was a parking space, although it left a very narrow gap for cars to get past.

"Stay with Bertha in case you have to move her," Tank said. "We won't be long."

Dale was a little disappointed at not getting a chance to meet the lord of the manor again. Despite their rocky first meeting, the man was very easy on the eye. Thinking about Ben Raleigh occupied Dale, and he jumped when he heard a loud horn. A dustcart trundled down the road toward him. Dale knew the dustcart wouldn't manage to get by Bertha. He was about to move when Emma rapped on the window.

"Back her up towards the pole. It doesn't matter if she goes on the grass."

Dale waved at the dustcart to indicate he was going to move and carefully backed up. He was so busy concentrating on not clipping the cars as he maneuvered that he forgot what was behind him. Suddenly, he heard a screeching sound and then a horrible crash.

Dale leaped out of the engine and rushed around the back, not surprised to see Tank and Keith, plus a handful of others, gathered around a pole. *Oh shit! The* pole. The bloody maypole. Dale had managed to knock over the maypole covered in blue, white, and red ribbons. It didn't matter how many times he said it inside his head, the pole was on the ground and they were all staring at him.

"You…. You…." Lord Calminster took a step forward, his eyes flashing and his fists clenched.

Dale stepped back, not sure if Lord Calminster was going to take a swing at him or not. "Fuck, I'm sorry. I didn't see the pole."

If anything, this seemed to inflame the man even more. "It's a twelve-foot pole covered in red and blue ribbons. How could you not see it?"

Good question. Dale had no idea.

"Fuck me," Tank muttered. "You've done it now. He's going to kill you."

"Can't we replace the pole? I mean, how often is it used?"

His lordship stared at him with an icy expression. "This pole has been here for over a hundred years. It was erected by my great-grandfather."

Yeah, Dale had fucked up. He got that. Although he was trying not to kill himself laughing at the thought of erecting poles. This was not the time for a sense of humor. Dale was so dead. And possibly unemployed and homeless as well. He glared at the rest of the crew, standing around like useless lumps.

Then Mrs. Manning rushed over. "Oh my goodness, Mr. Ben, what happened to the maypole? The whole village will be here for the May Day parade. What are the kids going to dance around now?"

Dale took a deep breath and focused his attention on Lord Calminster, whose expression was now positively thunderous. "I'm sorry, your lordship. This is all my fault. I'll fix the maypole. It should be fine by the May Day parade. As none of the crew warned me, they can help." He scowled at Tank, Keith, and Mick.

"And where are the kids supposed to practice while you do this?" Ben snapped.

They could wrap the bloody ribbons around his lordship for all Dale cared. He'd apologized and offered a solution; what more did the man want? He snapped his mouth shut before he said what he thought.

"They could practice around a tree," Mrs. Manning said hesitantly. "Just until the post is up."

Ben's scowl deepened, but he nodded. "I expect the fire department to be out here tomorrow morning to replace the maypole."

"Yes, sir." Tank's hand twitched, as if he wanted to tug his forelock. Not that Dale still had any clue what a forelock was, but Tank was all *yes, sir, no, sir* around Lord Benedict bloody Calminster.

"Let's get the business dealt with so you can leave before you do any more damage." Ben stalked off.

"You stay here," Tank said to Dale. "The rest of you, come with me."

Dale huffed as they walked off, leaving him alone with Mrs. Manning. He huffed again and then realized he was being a dick, considering he'd just ruined her hard work. "I'm really sorry, Mrs. Manning. I promise you everything will be fixed for the parade."

She gave him a forced smile. "I know it will, dear. Just make sure it's done right. Lord Calminster is very particular, and he will be very upset if the pole falls over during the parade."

Dale refrained from saying where he'd like to stick the bloody pole and smiled apologetically again. "We'll do it right. The pole will be there for another hundred years." He walked over to inspect the wood, lying splintered and bedraggled on the grass. "I think we'd better paint it as well. I don't think his lordship would appreciate fire-engine red up his nice white pole." He was sure he heard a snicker from Mrs. Manning, but she didn't say anything other than agreeing with him. "I don't know anything about this parade. Do you have a few minutes to tell me about it?"

He'd obviously said the right thing, because her eyes lit up, and for the next half an hour Mrs. Manning told him the entire history of the May Day celebrations at Calminster Hall. By the end of her speech, Dale's brain had dribbled out of his ears, but he did know far more about how important the May Day parade was to the village.

Just as she finished, Tank and the others reappeared, although there was no sign of Lord Calminster. Dale grinned at Tank. "Is his lordship going to put me in the stocks?"

"Not today, although I ought to warn you he has an entire room filled with instruments of torture, so don't piss him off again. Pardon me, ma'am." Tank apologized to Mrs. Manning.

"That's quite all right, Tank," Mrs. Manning said. "He has been known to threaten people who annoy him with the rack."

"You're joking," Dale said.

Mrs. Manning shook her head. "Oh no, he really does. I don't think he's actually used any of them yet, but there is always a first time."

"The next thing you'll be telling me is that there is a dungeon under the Hall."

"Two, actually," Mrs. Manning said cheerfully.

Dale shook his head. "I'll remember that the next time I upset his lordship."

"You going for a third time, Maloney? Isn't accusing him of criminal negligence and damaging his property enough?" Tank pointed to the fallen erection. "We've got to be here tomorrow morning at nine to replace the pole. And we have to paint it and repair any other damage around it."

"This young man has already said he would paint it," Mrs. Manning said.

"He's also got to arrange for the repairs to the engine," Tank said. "Fang is going to do his nut when he sees the white paint and the dent."

Dale had forgotten all about poor old Bertha. "I wish I hadn't got up this morning."

Keith clapped him on the back. "Don't worry, mate. My first week out, I backed into the station commander's car."

"You're joking?" Dale said.

Tank shook his head. "Why do you think we don't let him drive the engine anymore? The station commander was livid. He'd only had the car for a couple of days when Keith decided to flatten it."

"At least we can repair the pole. The car was flatter than a pancake. Japanese piece of shit. Sorry, ma'am," Keith added hastily.

"Yes, well, I think I ought to be heading back to the village," Mrs. Manning said. "I'll see you here tomorrow morning."

"Are you going to trust me to drive back?" Dale asked Tank.

His watch commander smirked. "If you promise to stay away from all stationary objects."

"Ha bloody ha. You're such a funny man." Dale got into the driver's seat and waited for everybody else to seat themselves. As he drove carefully down the narrow road, he noticed Lord Calminster standing near the edge of the trees. Dale tightened his hands on the wheel, paranoid that another suicidal pole was going to leap out into his path. In the rearview mirror, Dale could see Lord Calminster staring after them, and he growled under his breath. Not the next meeting he would have wanted with his landlord. At least he knew now to avoid him.

BACK at the station, Dale had to confess to the station commander about the unfortunate incident with the pole. Fang groaned as Tank described what had happened.

"In front of Lord Calminster? Jesus, Maloney, do you have a death wish? You do realize that his lordship's never going to let us forget it?"

"I know," Dale said. "I'm sorry, sir. I just didn't see the pole."

"Do you need an eye test, Maloney?"

"Yes, sir," Dale said automatically. "I mean, no, sir."

Fang rolled his eyes. "How did his lordship take it?"

Tank chuckled, taking far too much pleasure in Dale's discomfiture. "We've got to go back tomorrow to replace the pole, and then we have to paint it. One side is a lovely shade of fire-engine red."

"Let's inspect poor old Bertha," Fang said.

"There's a small dent and a lot of white paint," Dale said as he led the way. "It'll take more than an old pole to damage this girl."

"Do you know how much paperwork there's going to be?" Fang studied the damage to the appliance. "I guess it's not that bad. It's not as bad as Keith's attempt to destroy my car. Still, this is not a good start, Dale."

Dale resisted the desire to scuff the floor like a little boy. "I'm sorry, sir. I'll sort the pole out and repaint it out of my own pocket."

"Don't be daft. We'll do this by the book. Besides, it will give you lot something useful to do tomorrow instead of hanging around the station getting fat."

"We're not fat!" Tank sounded very offended at the thought.

Fang snorted, and then he turned to Dale, with a resigned expression. "Come on, let's get the paperwork over and done with."

Dale sighed and followed the station commander back into his office. He hated paperwork at the best of times.

WHEN Dale arrived for his shift the next day, the first thing he noticed was the bright red L-plate on his locker door. He rolled his eyes and opened his locker. He'd expected something of the sort to happen.

"Red Watch heard about your little accident," Mick said as he got changed into his uniform. "Don't expect that to be the last."

Dale shrugged his shoulders. "I can take whatever they give out."

"Good man. Just let me know if it gets too much. The fuckers can go too far sometimes."

As they were on their own, Dale took the opportunity to ask Mick something that had been on his mind. "You guys don't seem to care that I'm gay."

Mick didn't seem surprised by the question. "White Watch is okay. Stay away from Woody from Red. He'll give you a lecture on the spread of AIDS. And Dingbat from Blue. Definitely stay away from him. He used to be a Hell's Angel, then he caught religion."

"You don't like churchgoers?"

"I don't really care what you believe in, but Dingbat knocks on doors. He knocked on my door once, asking me to invite Jesus into my life. I invited him and Jesus in for a gay orgy. He's not spoken to me since."

Dale stared at Mick, who winked at him. "You're joking!"

"Go and ask him. Tell him you're gay too. He'll either quote Bible verses at you or run like hell."

"So what's Woodcote's problem?"

Mick sobered up. "His sister died of AIDS. She caught it from an ex-boyfriend who didn't keep his dick wrapped up. By the time she found out, it was too late. Woody's never really recovered."

"Damn, that's sad. Poor man."

"Yeah, but he ain't too keen on poofters. His words, not mine," Mick added hastily.

Dale sighed, but he said, "Thanks for the warning. I'll stay away from both of them."

"No one else gives a shit, or if they do, they keep it to themselves. The worst you'll get is this." He pointed at the L-plate.

Dale could handle himself, and he wasn't fussed about a bit of hazing, but he was glad he'd had the chat with Mick. There were another couple of L-plates on Bertha. Conscious of the rest of the watch huddled like a group of naughty schoolboys in the kitchen doorway, Dale removed the plates and stuck them in the cab; then he smirked at the guys.

"You going to stand there all day?"

Keith seemed disappointed at Dale's lack of reaction, but the rest just shrugged and wandered over.

The first job of the day was repairing the maypole. Dale found himself driving back to Calminster Hall. He had offered to let someone else drive, but Tank told him to shut up and get behind the wheel, although Tank moaned all the way to the village green that Dale drove even slower.

As Dale pulled up to where the maypole was lying on the ground, he could see Lord Calminster. He had three dogs milling around his feet, a Yorkie and two larger varieties, although Dale didn't have a clue what breed. He would have liked to say hello to the dogs, but from the way his lordship was glaring at Dale, he decided it was a bad idea.

"This is going to be a very long day," Dale muttered.

"You have no idea," Tank said. "His lordship is going to stand there and watch us work. He's a perfectionist."

Keith snorted. "You mean he's an OCD bastard."

Dale's heart sank. "I really hope you're kidding."

"I wish he was," Tank said. "But he will make sure it's done to his standards or we'll have to do it all over again."

Dale felt guilty about subjecting them to Lord bloody Calminster, and he said so, but Mick just laughed. "It's better than the exercise drills the commander had planned, and his lordship's not that bad. He just likes things being done a certain way."

"Come on, then." Tank jumped down from Bertha's cab, and everybody else followed him.

Dale hung back as Tank went to speak to Lord Calminster, who seemed to have a permanent scowl fixed to his face. He reminded Dale of the heroes on his mother's romance novels—impossibly handsome men with impossibly pretty women attached to their chests. Dale sighed inwardly. He wouldn't mind having his lordship attached to him, but it would be somewhere south of his navel. Not that that was liable to happen, now that Dale had "destroyed a piece of Calminster Hall's history."

"Okay, guys," Tank said. "We're going to dig out a new hole, replace the old pole with that one over there"— he pointed to a large wooden pole on one side—"paint it, fix the ribbons to the pole, and repair the old hole."

"I'll be back later to see how you're getting on," Lord Calminster said.

"Righto," Tank said cheerfully.

Dale breathed a sigh of relief when Lord Calminster stalked away without saying anything to him, his dogs hard on his heels. "I'll dig a hole, as it was my fault this happened."

"Don't be daft," Mick said. "It was all our faults. None of us banged on Bertha to stop you. Including his lordship."

That was a very good point, Dale thought. They had all watched him demolish a piece of Calminster Hall's history without a single yell. Nevertheless, he got the spades from Bertha and started digging a hole exactly where Tank pointed. It would be just his luck if he dug the hole in the wrong place. He almost expected his bloody Lordship to return with a tape measure and a spirit level.

After a couple of hours, Lord Calminster did return with the dogs, carrying two large bags. Instead of a tape measure, he produced bottles of ice-cold water, the condensation running down the sides, and huge sugary jam doughnuts.

"It's a hot day for March," Lord Calminster said as he handed them out, "and I thought you might be thirsty. I know what Tank's like if he doesn't get his doughnuts."

Everyone gave startled, polite laughs, as if they were amazed he had a sense of humor. Ben offered water and jam doughnuts to everyone, including Dale; then he said, "I'll take the coffee order now."

"You don't have to do that," Tank said. "We can go across to the tearooms and pick up coffee."

Lord Calminster held up his hand. "Call it my thanks for repairing this so quickly."

"I'm so sorry for knocking down the pole," Dale said, speaking to Lord Calminster for the first time since yesterday.

"Mrs. Manning pointed out to me in no uncertain terms that no one tried to stop you reversing into the pole," Lord Calminster said. "We all stood there like lemons and watched you."

Tank chuckled, saying, "We've just had that conversation."

Lord Calminster smiled briefly. "Anyway, what would you like, coffee or tea?"

The dogs sniffed around everyone, obviously in hope of one of them dropping their doughnut, but they were doomed to disappointment. As the other men gave their orders, Dale took the opportunity to give the dogs a rub behind the ears, and when he raised his head, Ben was smiling at him. Dale, who'd cursed Lord Calminster's name, rank, and serial number as he'd dug out the hole, felt unaccountably warm under Ben's gaze. He wanted to drown in Lord Calminster's blue eyes—

"Mr. Maloney?"

"Huh?" Dale suddenly realized Lord Calminster was talking to him.

"What do you want to drink?" Lord Calminster asked patiently.

"Uh… tea… thanks." Dale's cheeks heated. He'd managed to make a fool of himself again.

Lord Calminster smiled at him as if he hadn't noticed Dale's embarrassment. They stared at each other, just long enough for it to be awkward; then Calminster whistled at the dogs and walked away. Two of the dogs followed him, one of the larger ones bouncing off in pursuit of a squirrel.

"Don't get too interested," Tank murmured in Dale's ear.

"What?" Dale dragged his gaze away from Calminster.

"Just because he's being all friendly now, he's the lord of the manor, and he doesn't mix with the rest of us. Got his own social circle full of blondes and money."

Fuck! Was I that obvious?

Dale tried to laugh it off. "He's pretty to look at."

Tank clapped him on the back, nearly driving Dale to his knees. "Pretty? If you say so. I prefer something more—" He outlined the obvious shape of a woman.

Dale shook his head. "They're all yours, mate." He preferred his lovers just like… *shit*… Lord Calminster.

Chapter Four

AFTER the hot drinks had been dispensed, Ben said farewell, knowing his accounts wouldn't wait any longer. He whistled for the dogs, who joined him reluctantly, and walked across the green toward the trees. Hidden in the shadow of the beech trees at the edge of the green, Ben turned back one last time, to see Maloney stretch and roll his shoulders.

Damn, what a sight! Maloney's T-shirt had ridden up and displayed a thin layer of his flat belly as he stretched. Ben's mouth watered at the thick line of dark hair disappearing into his waistband. He reluctantly raised his gaze from the treasure trail to see Dale staring back at him.

Ben flushed and turned on his heel. He scurried back to the Hall as though all the hounds of hell were after him. Back in his study, he flung himself into his chair and knocked his head against his desk, highly embarrassed to have been caught staring at the new firefighter. He thought he had been sufficiently hidden from view. Ben knocked his head again and sat up, as it occurred to him that he hadn't been the only one staring. Dale had also been staring back at him.

Ben took a deep breath. It didn't matter who was staring at whom. Dale was a handsome man, but that was all. He didn't probe too deeply that suddenly Maloney had become Dale in his mind. He decided to put the man out of his thoughts altogether and tried to focus on the accounts, although he had to admit he kept straying to his brief glimpse of the treasure trail as Dale stretched.

It was almost a relief when someone knocked an hour later. The dogs raised their heads in anticipation.

Colson poked his head around the door. "Lunch is ready, sir. And the watch commander called to say they're done."

"Were there any problems?"

"No problems. They've taken the ribbons. When the pole is dry, they'll replace them."

Ben smiled at him. "Thank you, Colson. I'll be down in a moment."

Colson shut the door, leaving Ben alone with his less-than-pure thoughts. Perhaps Ben ought to insist Dale fix the ribbons. There might be some stretching involved.

One of the things that was foremost in his mind—aside from Dale Maloney—was his strained relationship with Sabrina. She was the daughter of one of his business partners, and a beautiful and clever woman. He knew it was expected that he would make an offer for her hand in marriage soon, as it would make sense to merge the businesses. However, marrying Sabrina was the last thing

Ben wanted to do. He also knew that Sabrina had guessed about his lack of interest in her, because she had been pressing him for a "talk," and he had been avoiding the subject. Their relationship had been confined to dinner dates and the occasional weekend away, but they hadn't taken it into the bedroom. Ben had pleaded a desire to take it slowly, but he knew she was growing impatient to move it to the next stage. He couldn't blame her, and he knew he was going to have to do something very soon before it imploded in his face. He could take a knock to his business, because he had fingers in many pies. But a knock to his personal reputation would be something else entirely.

Ben had been stupid to think he could maintain a relationship with a woman. He had no desire to kiss her, and even less to have a sexual connection. He wanted heirs to inherit Calminster Hall, but he was swiftly coming to realize he couldn't do it the conventional way. Just the sight of Dale Maloney, and the effect he had on Ben's body, made Ben realize he had to do something about Sabrina, and soon.

He flicked open his phone and tapped a number. Sabrina's elegant face appeared. She had put this particular image into his phone to remind him of her. Ben sighed loudly. He didn't need her photo; she was spectacular enough without it. Spectacular or not, she wasn't the one for him, and he needed to man up and talk to her.

"Hello, darling." Her voice was like silk over pebbles, a contradiction that had many men panting—apparently. Ben preferred a deeper, gravelly voice.

"Sabrina, you wanted to talk," he said brusquely.

"Finally."

"Would you like to come to dinner tonight?"

"I think I would prefer a more neutral territory," she said. "We could go to Chez Jacques."

Ben sighed. The last thing he wanted to do was play out a deep and meaningful conversation in public, but at least if they talked in public, there would be less amateur dramatics.

"Is eight o'clock all right? I'll book the table."

"I'll see you there," she said coolly.

Usually he would offer to pick her up, but this time he didn't. It was better if she guessed this was a serious conversation and what the potential outcome was. He said goodbye and disconnected the call. Any hope of focusing on his accounts went out of the window as Ben thought about what he was going to say to Sabrina. After several futile minutes staring at the numbers on the screen, he gave up and went out the double doors to stand on the veranda overlooking the formal gardens.

Sabrina would be upset, he knew that, but it was better for both of them if she knew there was no hope of a serious relationship. He wondered how her father was going to react. Thomas Barrett was a bombastic type, and he wouldn't be happy at anyone upsetting his little girl, or his plans. Ben didn't have to wonder too hard which would upset Barrett the most.

Even as Ben thought about the forthcoming conversations, he couldn't help the image of Dale Maloney slipping into his mind. The man was fucking hot, and Ben had a feeling—hoped—Dale was also gay, otherwise he could be in a lot of trouble.

Ben raised his gaze to the blue skies above. "Oh God, please, let Dale Maloney be gay."

HE arrived at Chez Jacques a little before eight o'clock. It didn't surprise him that he was the first to arrive. Sabrina had a habit of being late whatever the event. Ben followed the maître d' to his table and ordered a glass of pinot noir while he waited. Sabrina arrived about fifteen minutes later, all eyes following her as she was led to his table. Normally she would be full of apologies and air kisses, but this time she just gave him her hand and sat down. Beyond a brief hello, she barely spoke to him. Ben offered Sabrina a glass of wine, which she accepted, and then they ordered, so familiar with the menu they didn't bother to glance at it.

Sabrina sipped at her wine, obviously waiting for Ben to start the conversation.

Ben set the menu aside and took a deep breath. "I owe you an apology." Ben wanted to chew on his nail, a nervous gesture, but he kept his hands on the table.

She stared at him, and Ben noticed a small clump of mascara in one corner of her eye. "What's going on, Ben? You've barely spoken to me in weeks."

"I've been distracted."

"You've been avoiding me," Sabrina corrected.

Ben decided to ignore that, even if she was correct. "I know you've been frustrated by my—uh—lack of affection lately."

Sabrina raised one perfectly arched eyebrow. "Lately?"

"At all," Ben amended.

"So what do you plan to do about it?"

Ben took a deep breath. "I think we should end our relationship."

"End our relationship?" From her incredulous expression, splitting up had been the last thing on her mind. "You're dumping me?"

Her voice rose at the end of the sentence, and Ben cringed inwardly. This was why he'd wanted to talk privately, but he couldn't take the words back.

"I think it would be better."

Sabrina's eyes were so wide her eyebrows vanished under her fringe, and she fixed him with a glare. "Why do you want to split up?"

Ben stared at his glass of wine for a long moment before he spoke. "I agreed to go out with you because your father insisted it would be a good idea."

"I know that," she said. "My father thinks it would be a good idea for us to merge companies, and marriage is his way of organizing that."

"You know that's what he wants?" Ben hadn't realized Sabrina had been aware of her father's machinations.

"Of course I know," Sabrina said impatiently. "He's been dying to get his hands on the Calminster estate for years. I thought you were aware of this. Isn't that why you agreed to the merger?"

Ben leaned back in his chair and gave her an icy stare. "I think the merger of parts of our companies would be a good idea, but your father is sadly mistaken if he thinks he is going to get his hands on the estate and its businesses."

Sabrina studied him with renewed interest. Her anger at being dumped seemed to have faded away. She opened her mouth to speak, pausing as a waiter approached with an offer to pour them more wine.

When he was gone, she said, "I didn't want to get married to you in the first place."

"You didn't want to date me?" Ben was surprised. She'd seemed very enthusiastic at the idea of their relationship.

"I didn't mind dating you. You're a pleasurable companion, and I've had fun with you. But you're an awfully dull lover. If you don't want to move the relationship into the bedroom, I don't see any point in staying together." Sabrina eyed him speculatively. "So who is he?"

Ben choked on his wine. "What do you mean?"

At least she waited until he'd stopped coughing and wiped his eyes. "I'm not that stupid, Ben. I knew you were gay from the moment I met you, but my father insisted you must be bisexual, or you wouldn't have agreed to go out with me."

"Your father thinks I'm gay?" People from the other table turned their heads to their table as Ben raised his voice. He felt his cheeks warm, and he suddenly wished he were anywhere but there.

Sabrina shrugged expressively. "Daddy couldn't care less if you were gay or a monk, as long as you were prepared to marry me to do business."

Ben frowned as he thought about what she said. "What does that make you?"

"A commodity or a puppet," she said. Her tone was light, but Ben caught the edge of bitterness. "My father sees me as someone to be used, just like any other part of his empire. You're a commodity too."

"And now? What will he do now I've split up with you?" Ben was suddenly worried for her.

She waited until the food had been served. "I have plans. I think it's about time I reminded Daddy dearest I am not one of his commodities to be moved around. You know I'm a lawyer?"

"And a good one, from what I hear," Ben said.

"Daddy set me up with my own firm. A graduation present on the understanding I would always work for him."

"And if you defy him?"

"There is a board of directors who can remove me at any moment." Sabrina seemed remarkably sanguine about the situation.

Ben narrowed his eyes "So what have you done?"

She gave a wicked smile, and Ben was glad it wasn't aimed at him. "I founded a new firm of corporate lawyers, and my father doesn't know anything about it. I've been running both companies for several months while we set it up, but it's time I made a decision to focus on my own life."

"I don't know what to say," Ben admitted. "I thought you were your father's daughter."

Sabrina leaned forward and fixed him with her gaze. "I *am* my father's daughter, and you would do well to remember that. I am as clever, if not cleverer than he is. I know you need a new firm of lawyers. I know you've been searching."

"How do you know that?" Ben asked.

"Because you approached my new firm, Bradshaw, Logan, and Winslet. Bradshaw was my mother's name."

Ben shut his mouth, aware he was gaping at her, and she chuckled.

"I think this is the most emotion I've seen out of you in nine months of dating. I like it, Ben. I'm the best there is. I'm more than a match for my father."

Ben picked at an asparagus spear on his plate. "You amaze me. I thought…." He trailed off, not sure how to phrase his next words.

Sabrina shrugged again. "As I said, I knew or at least suspected you were gay. At least now I know it was all you and not me." The smile on her face showed him she was trying to be honest and not a bitch. Ben had to give her that one. Sabrina was a stunning woman, and if he weren't gay, then he might have been attracted to her. He had a feeling she wouldn't mind being dominant in the bedroom. "Have you met someone else?"

Ben stared at her. "What makes you think that?"

"You'd never have had the balls to split up with me otherwise."

"You believe in sticking the knife in, don't you?"

She gave an elegant shrug. "I'm a lawyer. It's my job. So?"

"I've met someone," he admitted. "Although I've only seen him once or twice."

"Well, which is it? Once or twice?"

"Twice, although the first time was under difficult circumstances." Ben grinned at her. "He rescued Mrs. Wilson and accused me of negligence. The second time wasn't much better. He knocked down the village maypole." For a minute he thought he was going to have to explain to Sabrina what a maypole was, and then she burst out laughing.

"You've fallen for the fireman."

Ben blinked. "How did you hear about that?"

"I told you, I know everything. However, in this instance I met someone from the village, who told me all about the maypole incident."

"You have spies everywhere."

"Why do you think my father and I have been so successful?"

"You're scary, you know that?"

Sabrina sipped wine delicately and smirked at Ben. "You have no idea, Ben. You are a minnow compared to my family of sharks."

Ben was sure he had just had a lucky escape; however, he still had two things to deal with. "I will arrange to retain Bradshaw, Logan, and Winslet tomorrow morning, and I will talk to your father. I am still interested in merging part of Calminster Enterprises with his firm, but he can keep his sticky hands off my estate. If you are interested in working *for* me"—and he emphasized the "for"—"you may end up going against your father. Are you prepared for that? I don't want to find myself being maneuvered in a different way. I'm not going to be your puppet to upset your father."

"I have been preparing for this moment my entire life," Sabrina said. "You won't regret changing to our firm."

"I'd better not." Ben took a large swallow of wine and thought about ordering another bottle. Hell, he could call Colson to send out someone to pick him up. "How about a bottle of champagne to celebrate our new working partnership?"

"Why not?" she agreed. "And congratulations, on taking one foot out of the closet."

"This is still new to me. I'd appreciate it if you didn't spread the news around."

Sabrina mimed zipping her lipsticked mouth. "Your secret is safe with me. Although, if you start fucking the fireman, I don't suppose it will stay quiet for very long."

Ben wasn't sure what shocked him the most—the news that she was not under the thumb of her father, or the swear word out of her pretty mouth. Maybe he was a little naïve. He caught the waiter's eye, really needing a glass of champagne.

Chapter Five

DALE moaned as a ray of sunlight penetrated his dreamless slumber. He rolled over and tried to get back to sleep, as this was his first day off after four days on shift, but it was futile. It was impossible for him to relax enough to drift off again. Dale opened his eyes and stared up at the ceiling, noticing the cobweb in the corner had become larger overnight. The spider had made itself known on Dale's first night. Dale didn't like spiders, but he wasn't frightened of them either, and he had suggested to the spider that they could live together if the spider kept out of Dale's way. So far their relationship seemed to be quite harmonious.

"Stay in your corner, Charlie," he muttered, but the spider didn't react.

Finally, grumbling in disgust at himself for waking up so early, Dale rolled out of bed and headed down the narrow stairs to the bathroom. He switched on the kettle on the way past, as it was an old cottage and the bathroom was accessed through the kitchen. Dale relieved himself and brushed his teeth, then headed back to the kitchen to make a cup of tea.

Once he'd made the drink, Dale curled up in the corner of his sofa and switched on the news. It must have been a slow news day, as the headlines were dominated by a group of celebrities Dale had never heard about. He was the first to admit he knew nothing about celebrity culture. Dale only read the sports pages of the newspapers and was useless when people tried to get him on pub quiz teams. Baz had bitched constantly that Dale had no idea who anybody was after 2005.

Dale decided to go for a run instead and explore the local area. Since he had arrived, Dale had either worked or slept. His shifts weren't conducive to a social life. It had never mattered that much when he lived with Baz, but now the loneliness was beginning to eat at his soul.

The weather was still cool enough to make running pleasurable at that time in the morning, and Dale set off toward the village green. Okay, he admitted to himself, maybe he ran in that direction in the hope of bumping into the lord of the manor. He had heard that Ben worked long hours and was seldom seen in the village. Still, one could hope, and Dale was nothing if not optimistic.

Dale felt a twinge in his right calf, and he realized he had not spent enough time warming up. He decided to take things slowly rather than risk doing more damage. As he approached the village green, he could see the maypole, with the bound ribbons fluttering slightly in the

The Fireman's Pole

breeze. He pulled a face, thinking about the grief he had received since knocking the pole to the ground. His crew hadn't let him forget it, and even in the village shops, it was still mentioned every time he walked in. Dale took it all in good spirits, but he would be glad when life quieted down a bit. He decided to run around the green, knowing what he really meant was he hoped he would see Ben.

The good spirits were obviously listening, because he had only made half a circuit when Ben almost bumped into him as he emerged from the trees. Dale stopped suddenly, catching Ben by the arms before he crashed to the ground.

"Can't you look where you're going?" Ben snapped as he recovered his balance. His scowl was so fierce, Dale stepped back.

"You stepped out on me. I stopped just in time, otherwise you'd be on your arse," Dale pointed out as mildly as he could. Ben glared, then pushed past without another word. Dale felt his hackles rise and couldn't resist yelling "You're welcome" after him.

Ben's back radiated anger as he made his way across the green toward the village and Dale sighed. Their meeting hadn't been the one he'd been hoping for. He knew there was a sparkle of electricity between them, but Ben seemed in a permanently bad mood. Then he noticed Ben had turned on his heel and was walking back toward him, still with the scowl plastered to his face. Dale was tempted to run on, but he waited for Ben to join him.

"I'm sorry," Ben said as soon as he was in hearing range. "I've had a bad morning, but I shouldn't have taken it out on you." His apology was sincere, even if his tone was short.

"Is there anything I can do to help?" Dale asked.

"I wish." Ben sounded rueful rather than angry. "Got any suggestions for dealing with a business shark?"

Business and sharks were outside of Dale's remit, but he studied the slump in Ben's shoulders and decided to take a chance. "Where were you going before we crashed into each other?"

"To get some chocolate," Ben said.

"Do you have time for a cup of coffee?"

Ben seemed surprised by the offer. "Not long, because I've got a meeting."

"Have you got half an hour?"

"I can do that."

Dale beamed at him, and Ben blinked as if he were dazzled. "Where're your dogs?"

"Gone for a long run with one of the gardeners." Ben smiled at him. "Tim loves dogs but his mum won't let him have one, so he borrows mine."

As they walked toward the coffee shop, Dale suddenly remembered he didn't have any money on him. "Damn!"

"What's wrong?"

"I wasn't expecting to do anything like this," Dale said. "I left my wallet at home. Can we swing by the cottage to pick it up?"

"I think I can pay for a cup of coffee," Ben said.

Knowing Ben had limited time, Dale said, "Okay, you buy this time, and I'll buy the next one."

"You seem so sure there'll be a next one."

Dale was kind of shocked by Ben's teasing tone, but he waggled his eyebrows. "You mean there won't be?"

"I think we'll see how this one goes," Ben said quietly.

Dale winked at him and smirked at the flush on Ben's cheeks. The chatter in the café ceased as they walked in, and Dale was conscious of the surprised and speculative glances from everyone. Except the old man in the corner. He didn't raise his head from the racing pages of his newspaper. One of the women hurried around to greet them.

"Lord Calminster, good morning. How are you?"

Ben shook her hand. "Morning, Mrs. Rollins. We're just stopping for a cup of tea."

"Good to see you. Come and sit over here."

She led Ben to the table in the window. From the way she fussed over him, Ben was obviously a celebrity in the village.

"Do you get this attention outside of Calminster?" Dale asked once they'd sat down and she'd left them alone. He was conscious of the constant glances their way, even if the conversation had started again.

"Only when I start flashing my *Lord Muckety-Muck* title around," Ben teased, reminding Dale of their first conversation.

"I get the same thing when I tell people I'm a firefighter," Dale said.

Ben's eyes opened wide, and then he realized Dale was joking. "It's the uniform, isn't it? It has that effect on women."

"And men too." Dale decided if Ben was fishing, Dale might as well give him the answer he was fishing for.

Ben didn't raise his eyes from the menu, but Dale knew he had got the message by the way his hands shook.

Dale studied Ben's hands. Nice, strong, masculine hands, with long fingers. Good hands. He suddenly had visions of those hands wrapped around his cock. Dale knew he had to put those thoughts well away from his head while he was wearing shorts that hid nothing. He recited the seven-times table in his head to calm things down, but when he saw Ben was discreetly studying him, the numbers flew out of his head. They locked gazes on each other for a long moment, and Dale wondered how they didn't set the chintz tablecloth on fire.

A cough interrupted them, and Dale glanced up to see a young lad with bad acne holding a notebook and blushing wildly.

"Um… I'm sorry, but do you know what you want to order?"

Ben smiled at the lad, who, to Dale's amusement, blushed even deeper. "I would like… er… a pot of Earl Grey tea and two slices of toast—granary bread, I think. Thanks, Patrick." He smiled at Dale. "What would you like?"

"I'll have a pot of normal tea and toast. Make it white bread, please." Dale stuffed the menu in its holder and waited until Patrick had gone before he said, "Do you know our waiter?"

"Patrick's worked on the estate before. I take on a lot of local teenagers over the summer to give them something to do. It helps their parents who have to go out to work." Dale shook his head, and Ben said, "What's the matter?"

"You have a big heart."

Ben reddened, obviously embarrassed by Dale's declaration. "Not really. It's a practical thing to do. Otherwise they'd be roaming around in packs, seeking out trouble. It's not like any of them want to work on the estate. They'd rather be on their computers or iPads. Their parents give them no choice."

Dale rumbled a laugh, and a few people from the other tables glanced over, bright curiosity in their eyes. They averted their gaze when Dale stared at them. "I like that." He leaned forward and lowered his voice. "I like you."

And that had to be the time Patrick returned with their tea and toast. This time all three of them had wildly flushing cheeks. They said nothing until Patrick poured the tea and left them alone.

Ben lifted his cup and paused. "I like you too."

"Even if I did demolish part of your history?" Dale smirked at him before he took a sip, trying to hold back a grimace. The tea could have done with a lot longer in the pot.

"My great-grandfather would be turning in his grave," Ben said solemnly. "He erected that pole with his own two hands."

"Really?"

Ben snickered, and Dale realized he'd been taken for a ride. "Of course he didn't. My great-grandfather had a house full of servants and didn't lift a finger if he could get away with it. He nearly bankrupted the estate, and it was only thanks to the skill of my father that we still have the house."

"And now you."

Ben furrowed his brow. "What do you mean?"

"From what I hear, you've doubled the income on the estate."

"I think we'll find I've quadrupled the income."

Dale shook his head. "I can't imagine the amount of work it must take to run a place like Calminster Hall and make money. Aren't most stately homes given to the National Trust these days?"

"It's just one of those things. What we did worked, and because of it, we can employ a lot of people."

Patrick approached them again. "Would you like a refill of tea?"

Ben glanced at his watch. Dale inwardly drooled at the fine hair curling around the black face. He had it so bad.

"I think I'd better get back home," Ben said. "Otherwise my estate manager will be sending out a search party."

Patrick retreated, and Dale stuffed the last bit of toast into his mouth, washing it down with tea. "Thank you for my breakfast."

"It was my pleasure," Ben said, and he really sounded as if he meant it, which made Dale feel better for having to mooch off him.

Ben paid the bill with a healthy tip for Patrick, and then they both left, blinking in the morning sunshine. Dale was a little cold, as he hadn't cooled down properly after his run.

They stood staring awkwardly at each other, and then Ben said, "I really have to go."

"Well," Dale said, "thanks again for breakfast, and I'll see you around."

Because the awkwardness was getting difficult, Dale turned and started to walk away, and then Ben said, "Stop!"

Dale glanced over his shoulder to see Ben jogging up to him. "Is everything okay?"

"Are you doing anything this afternoon?" Ben sounded breathless and a little unsure of what Dale's reaction would be to his offer.

"Not really. Maybe unpacking a little more, but aside from that, I haven't got anything planned."

"Would you like come to dinner?" The words came out in a rush.

"I thought Mrs. Wilson was still in hospital?" Dale said.

"She is, but I'm sure I can open a tin of beans."

"I love baked beans on toast," Dale said immediately and so enthusiastically that Ben smiled. "Especially with cheese on top."

"Great. Come over about three o'clock, and you can have a grand tour before dinner. I'll see if we've got any cheese."

"Three o'clock. See you then." Dale watched Ben walk away, and then he turned to run back to his house, albeit slowly. He didn't want to throw up after his breakfast.

Now he just had to decide what to do with himself until three o'clock that didn't involve working out what to wear.

Chapter Six

"NICE view!"

Ben sat up so sharply he banged his head on the desk, yelping loudly. "Ouch! Hell!" He backed out and turned on Dale. "What the hell are you doing here? Where's Colson?" He rubbed his head, his mood not improved by the smirk on Dale's face.

Dale's response was delayed by the dogs rushing him and demanding his attention, but when they stopped barking and licking him, he said, "You invited me, remember? Mr. Colson has gone to fetch afternoon tea. Seriously, you have afternoon tea? Mind my eye, mutt!" The last was a yelp as one of the larger dogs enthusiastically stuck a wet nose in his eye.

Ben scowled at Dale's open amusement. "Fluffy—careful. I always have afternoon tea. I did?"

"You don't remember inviting me to dinner? I'm wounded." He clutched a hand over his heart in an overly dramatic fashion.

"Arse! Dinner—yes. It's"—Ben squinted at the clock—"three. Shit, I said three, didn't I?"

"Sorry." Dale made an apologetic grimace. "Is it inconvenient? I can bugger off and come back later."

Ben huffed and rubbed at the bump on his head. "You don't have to do that. I've got an hour's paperwork left, but I'm sure I can find something for you to do after we have tea."

"Is this one really called Fluffy?" Dale scratched behind Fluffy's ears and he wriggled in ecstasy.

Ben sighed as Fluffy licked Dale's hand. Fluffy was almost the size of a Shetland pony. He was huge and hairy. "Blame the name on my sister. Fluffy was very, well, fluffy as a puppy. We had no idea he was going to grow so large. The Yorkie is called Frankie, and the other dog is Fern. Fluffy is Fern and Frankie's puppy."

Dale stared at little Frankie and then at Fluffy. "No fucking way."

"Believe me. We have no idea what happened there. Is Colson bringing tea?"

"Ah yes, Mr. Colson." Dale drawled out his name. "Your butler is a hottie."

"He is?" Ben asked, as if the thought had never occurred to him. "I don't really notice it. He's been here since I was a child, and his father was a butler before that."

"You really don't think your Mr. Colson's the hottest thing on two legs?"

Ben narrowed his eyes and glared at Dale. "You think Colson is the hottest thing on two legs?"

"Don't you?" Dale challenged, going on the offensive.

"He's my *butler*. Besides, he's not my type."

Dale stepped closer to Ben and ran a fingertip along Ben's jaw. "Who is your type?"

Ben swallowed hard, his Adam's apple bobbing. "You are," Ben admitted hoarsely.

Dale licked his lips and seemed about to get up close and personal, when someone knocked on the door. Dale barely had a moment to step back before the door opened and Colson came in, pushing a trolley. Ben didn't know whether to banish Colson or hug him for the interruption.

Ben led Dale to the armchairs by one of the open doors, where Colson was pouring the tea. He was pleased when Dale thanked Colson rather than ignoring him as some of Ben's friends were wont to do.

Dale waited until the butler had left and then grinned at him. "My mum will be so jealous when I tell her about this. Look at these sandwiches!"

As usual, the kitchen had provided them with small sandwiches with the crusts removed and cut into a triangle shape, and tiny cakes no more than a mouthful. Ben didn't like to tell Dale it was a joke between him and his staff. He didn't want to pop the bubble of enthusiasm. Although seeing the huge fireman holding a tiny sandwich between two fingers was kind of funny.

Ben damped down his smirk and asked, "Why would your mum be jealous?"

"She loves country houses. She dragged me around National Trust homes when I was a kid. I was bored witless and she had to bribe me with the promise of cake in the café."

"You'll have to bring her here. I'd be happy to take your mother on a tour." The delighted expression on Dale's face was enough for Ben's irritation at being caught head down and arse up to fade away.

"I'll be the favorite son forever! I'm the only son, but now I'll be the favorite only son." Dale was babbling, but Ben just raised an eyebrow and drank his tea. Dale sought for another topic of conversation. "I'd like to explore the gardens while you work. I only got as far as the green last time."

"As long as you don't decide to knock anything else down, you're welcome. I can get one of the grounds staff to show you around."

"I promise not to destroy anything else," Dale said. "I can explore by myself. I don't need the formal tour."

"All right, but I'll let them know you're here. Otherwise they'll call security." He saw the hint of surprise in Dale's eyes. "We have two security guards here and a professional security firm on standby. There are a lot of valuable items in the house."

Dale refused to meet his gaze. "I forget you're aristocracy."

Ben snorted. "Minor nobility at the most. It's just stuff, Dale."

"I was brought up on a council estate in south London." Dale waved his arm around the room. "This isn't stuff. The ornaments from Woolworths that I bought for Mum with my pocket money is stuff."

"I bet your mum loved the ornaments you bought her," Ben said.

"She said it was stuff she had to dust."

"All of this needs dusting too, and I have to pay people to do it."

"But—"

Ben hated the sudden inadequacy on Dale's face. It was an expression he'd seen his whole life. "Come with me. You guys stay here." He led Dale out of the study, shutting the door on the disappointed dogs. They went through the main hall and into a small room in the west wing. "This is my personal study. No one's allowed in here without my permission." Suppressing a sigh at Dale's intimidated expression, Ben pointed to a walnut-and-glass-fronted cabinet at the end of the room. "What do you see in there?"

Dale blinked, but he did what he was told. Ben watched him—okay, watched his arse—as Dale peered into the cabinet. Then Dale glanced over his shoulder, and Ben blushed at having been caught staring.

Dale smirked, but he said, "These are just like things I made as a kid."

"I made them, and so did my sister." He joined Dale at the cabinet and smiled fondly, remembering the hours he'd spent creating masterpieces out of clay, paper, and paint. "My mum kept all these."

"But you've got a house full of valuable antiques. Why on earth would your mum keep these?"

"Because the antiques meant nothing to her. They are heirlooms from my father's family. But these, these were made by her kids, and she loved them."

Dale stared at them a moment longer and then at Ben. "I think I would've liked your mum."

Ben blinked rapidly to hold back tears that threatened to spill over. "She would've liked you too." He found himself being enfolded in a one-armed hug by Dale, who said nothing but just held him for a moment. It was comforting; Dale smelled really nice—spicy and musky—and Ben had no desire to move.

All good things had to come to an end. At a knock on the door, Ben stepped back hastily. He thought he heard Dale sigh, but he said nothing as he let Ben go.

"Yes?" Ben called, aware there was a distinct snap in his voice.

"The estate manager is here for your meeting, your lordship."

Ben frowned. "Damn, I forgot about that. I'll be out in a minute."

"Yes, sir."

"I thought your butler calls you Mr. Ben," Dale said.

"He does, but not usually in front of strangers. Colson only calls me your lordship when there are people around." Ben rubbed his temples. "I'm so sorry. I've got to talk to Barry. Our meeting this morning got postponed."

"Not a problem. I'm the one who interrupted your afternoon. I'll go for a walk."

"The spring flowers are lovely this time of year," Ben said, opening the door of the study.

Dale tilted his head. "Do you like gardening?"

"Hate it," Ben confessed as they walked across the hall. "They're all weeds to me. The gardeners are under orders not to let me anywhere near the flowers. I only have to look at a plant and it dies."

"You can't be that bad," Dale said.

Ben ushered Dale into the large study. "I am, aren't I, Barry?"

The middle-aged estate manager looked confused. "You are what, your lordship?"

"Don't start that," Ben said. "This is Dale."

Barry raised an eyebrow. "The bloke that rescued Mrs. Wilson?"

"That's him. Dale, this is Barry Chalmers, Calminster Hall's estate manager."

To his surprise, Barry sprang to his feet and shook Dale's hand vigorously. "Thank you."

"You're welcome. What for?"

To Ben's amusement, Dale stuck his hand behind his back and flexed it a couple of times. Barry had a firm handshake.

"For finding Aunty Mavis," Barry said.

"Aunty… oh, Mrs. Wilson. She's your aunt?"

"She's not strictly my aunty, but as good as. She and my mum went to school together."

"I'm just glad I found her," Dale said. "She was almost hidden from view behind a wall."

Barry pumped Dale's hand again. "Don't be surprised if my mum turns up with biscuits and cakes at the fire station soon."

"I'm not going to complain," Dale assured him. Every fire station Dale had ever worked at loved supplies of homemade cakes and biscuits.

"As long as some of them come my way," Ben said plaintively.

"He's the hero," Barry said, pointing at Dale.

Dale puffed out his chest. "Yeah, I'm the hero. You wait your turn."

"But Barry's mum makes the best double chocolate chip cookies ever." Ben had seen grown men fight over the last cookie because they were that good.

The expression on Barry's face was as smug as if he were the one making the cookies. "She's the best in the village. She wins the prizes in the village fete every single year."

"I thought this was a parade." Dale was sure it was a parade and not a fete.

Barry turned to his boss. "You mean you haven't told him all about the village life?"

Ben hadn't had time to explain the ebb and flow of Calminster. But Dale was looking at him a little confused, and Barry obviously expected Ben to explain.

"We have three big events in the village during the year. In May we have the May Day parade, in September we have the cricket match combined with the village fete, and in November we have the Christmas Carnival."

Dale nodded. "So lots of competitions; gardens, cakes, and that sort of thing?"

"Don't ever make the mistake of thinking these aren't taken seriously," Barry said. "The villagers have been known to send people to Coventry for making that foolish error."

"I promise to keep my mouth shut," Dale said.

"Just praise everyone," Ben suggested. "Don't show any favoritism, unless it's Mrs. Wilson. And for heaven's sake, don't even think of entering any of the competitions. You have to be living in the village for at least fifty years to get a foot in the door."

Dale laughed, the laughter trailing off as both men stared back at him, deadly serious. "I hear you, and there's no fear of that. I have no baking skills."

Ben patted him on the arm, wishing he could grope the muscles longer. "You're golden in the eyes of the village. You rescued one of their matriarchs. Just smile, flex those muscles, and look pretty. That's all you need to do."

"I'm not sure whether to be insulted or not," Dale said. "Besides, I damaged part of the history of the village. People don't know whether to hug me or slap me. I'm the big bad hero, not pretty."

Ben would have loved to make a comment, but he refrained from embarrassing Barry. He could see the challenging expression on Dale's face, daring him to say something, but he just opened his eyes wide and kept his mouth shut. He took satisfaction in the disappointed glance Dale shot him. The one thing he really did need to do was have this meeting with Barry, and much as chatting with Dale was a good thing, it wasn't going to get the work done.

"I was just telling Dale about my black thumb," Ben said.

Barry chuckled. "Never let Mr. Ben near a plant. It'll be dead before he walks out of the room. He even managed to kill a cactus."

Dale seemed impressed. "How the heck did you manage to do that?"

"I overwatered it," Ben admitted.

"He's hopeless," Barry said, a large smile on his weathered face.

Dale pointed a finger at Ben. "Stay away from my orchids!"

Ben knew it was pathetic the way he reacted to the deep growl in Dale's voice. "Yes, sir." It didn't escape his notice that Barry's eyes widened. *Dammit*, Dale only had to be in the vicinity and Ben threw caution to the wind. Time to get things under control.

"I'll leave you to your meeting," Dale said. "Do you think the dogs would like to come for a walk?"

Ben nodded, fully aware from the way Dale had swayed toward him that he'd noticed the *yes, sir* as much as Barry had. "Barry, would you call security and the gardeners? Let them know we have a visitor."

Barry grabbed his walkie-talkie as Ben led Dale out onto the long veranda. Ben drew Dale out of Barry's sight and grabbed his hand. Dale stared at their joined hands and then at Ben, a question clearly in his expression.

"Be back here by five," Ben ordered.

"Yes, your lordship."

Ben threw caution to the wind and dragged Dale in for a kiss. It was the briefest brush of their mouths, but it was enough to make Ben want more.

He stepped back as he licked his lips, tasting sugar from the cakes. "Go now before I do something that will embarrass Barry."

Dale's lips twitched. He gave a mock salute, and whistling for the dogs, he vanished into the gardens, swiftly hidden by one of the hedges. With not even a backward glance at Ben, the traitors rushed to join him.

"You're supposed to be my dogs," Ben muttered before walking back into the study. To his relief, Barry said nothing beyond "Dale seems like a nice lad," although his eyes were conducting a whole other conversation.

"He is," Ben agreed, although Ben wasn't interested in the "nice" side of Dale. Not at all.

BY ten past five, Ben was ready to throw his laptop across the room. There was a mistake in one of the columns on his spreadsheet, but he couldn't work out where, and Dale was nowhere to be seen. Ben had told him to be back by five o'clock. Where the hell was he?

Ben heard voices outside the window, one of them definitely Dale's and both of them laughing. Ben stiffened, irrationally angry at Dale's happiness. Dale hadn't laughed like that, so free and easy, in Ben's company. He strode to the window to find Dale talking to one of the gardeners. Anger coiled in Ben's stomach as Dale made a deep belly laugh at something the gardener said. Tim was young, maybe twenty at the most, and one of the apprentices at the Hall. He was also blond, blue-eyed, and drop-dead gorgeous. It didn't take a rocket scientist to see Dale was attracted to him.

Then Dale noticed him and waved. Ben thought about ignoring him and walking back into the study, but he knew that would be petty and childish. Girding his loins, Ben pasted on a fake smile and joined the two men. He bent down to pet the dogs.

"Hello. You look like you've had more fun than me."

Dale grinned at him, his eyes twinkling in the sunshine. "I met up with Tim, and he showed me around. Tim's big brother went to my uni. I used to get drunk with him at the student union. I was just telling him some of Adam's secrets."

"I'm sure he'll appreciate that," Ben said dryly.

Tim laughed, although he seemed a little self-conscious now Ben was there. "He's been spilling my secrets my entire life. It will be good to get my own back."

"Don't forget to mention the one about wearing the pink bra and tied to the lamppost," Dale said, and he and Tim laughed, momentarily excluding Ben from the joke.

Ben was about to excuse himself and retreat to his study to lick his wounds when Dale turned to him.

"Are you free now?"

"More or less. Are you sure you don't want to continue with the tour?" Ben was proud of the way he kept the jealousy out of his voice.

Maybe he wasn't quite as successful as he hoped, because Dale narrowed his eyes and Tim shuffled his feet.

"I'd—er—better get on," Tim said, "or Joe'll have words."

Joe was the head gardener at Calminster Hall, with an extensive and salty vocabulary that he never failed to exercise.

"Thanks for your time," Dale said, clapping Tim on the back. Then Tim excused himself, and it was just the two of them.

Ben was about to speak when Dale got there first. "What's wrong?"

"Nothing's wrong," Ben lied.

"Then why do you look as if I killed your puppies?"

"I don't." Now Ben felt like an idiot.

"Yes, you do," Dale insisted. "You were fine when I left."

"You and Tim—"

"What about him?" Then Dale's eyes widened. "You were jealous of Tim?"

"No."

"You've got no reason to be jealous of him. He's totally straight. Got a girlfriend in the village." Now Ben felt embarrassed, even more so when Dale laughed. He should have known about Tim's girlfriend. He tried to avert his gaze but Dale cupped his jaw and made Ben focus on him. "She lives next door to me. Jenny's a nice girl. I told her I'd say hello if I saw Tim."

"You told your neighbor you were coming here?"

Dale nodded. "I said you invited me to look around the Hall. I know you're not out to the village. But I don't play games, Ben. I wouldn't come here and flirt with someone else."

"One of my exes used to," Ben said thinly.

"Then he's better off as an ex. My ex spent our entire relationship shagging women, and I never knew until I caught him in my bed with one of the women officers. She didn't know about me."

"You weren't out to the crew?"

Dale shook his head. "Baz was firmly in the closet. I didn't realize he kept it a secret so he could screw around."

"How long were you together?" Ben asked.

"Three years, nine months, and five days."

"You counted?"

Dale snorted. "You mean you don't know?"

"I do," Ben admitted with a wry smile. "Although none of them were long enough to deserve it."

"I know, and it fucking hurts that he cheated. I don't play games. Maybe I'm old-fashioned, but I'm faithful to my boyfriends." Dale knew it would take a long time for him to get over Baz's betrayal.

"How many have you had?"

Dale counted on his fingers. "Alf, Will, Paul, and Roland. Baz was the longest. What about you?"

"Hookups only, guys not wanting a public relationship," Ben said. "They were happy to keep it discreet."

"My crew know I'm gay. I'm not being shoved back in the closet again."

The silence hung between them crystalline sharp, and there was a warning in Dale's eyes. Still, he wasn't able to hoist the rainbow flag above Calminster Hall just yet.

"I need time."

"I can give you that," Dale said. "Much as I'd like to walk down Calminster High Street holding your hand, I don't think anyone is ready for that. I'm not sure I'm really ready *yet*." He emphasized the end word.

Ben shuddered at the thought. Calminster village definitely wasn't ready to see the lord of the manor parade down the street with another man—*yet*.

"On the other, if you should invite me to dinner…." Dale waggled his eyebrows.

"I've done that already," Ben pointed out.

"So you have. When's dinner?"

"I don't usually eat 'til seven."

Dale glanced at his watch. "That means we've got—an hour and a half until we eat."

"So?"

"I think it's time you showed me the house."

Ben stared at him. "You've just toured the garden and now you want a tour of the Hall?"

"I do."

"Are you a glutton for punishment?"

Dale stepped closer to Ben, into his personal space. "I thought we might find some dark corners."

Heat poured from the man. They weren't touching, but from the way Ben's body was reacting they might as well have been, "I think the Hall might have one or two."

"And you know where they are?"

Oh yes, Ben knew exactly where they were.

"Let's go, then."

Dale went to move away, but Ben grabbed his bicep. "There's something you've got to know. I don't play games either."

"Good to know." Dale took Ben's hand. "We need to find one of those dark corners."

"Why?" Ben asked stupidly.

"Because I'm going to kiss you."

"You could kiss me here," Ben pointed out.

Dale's smile was wicked. "I don't plan to make it a PG kind of kiss."

Despite Dale's heated words, he didn't seem anxious to get on with the kissing. He seemed content to go through the house as Ben gave him the visitor's tour. Ben was proud of his childhood home. He'd grown up with a history that stretched back centuries, and he'd always known that Calminster Hall would be his to hand down to his children. Even though he'd realized he was gay at an early age, Ben had accepted that he would have to get married at some point to have children, and despite the change in the marriage laws, he knew the only way to continue the line of Calminster would be by marrying "traditionally." Until his relationship with Sabrina, he'd accepted his marriage to a woman as part of his duty to the estate. However, his relationship with Sabrina had shown him that making love to a woman was impossible. Meeting Dale had been a wake-up call to Ben. Dale was a dose of oxygen in a world that had been filled with smog.

Dale asked intelligent questions as they went through the rooms, his childhood outings to stately homes obviously lending a degree of knowledge in styles and furnishings of the past.

As they discussed a rare Chippendale, Ben said, "Don't take this the wrong way, but I would never have guessed you grew up on a council estate."

"Because council house kids don't know anything about posh stuff, except to steal it?"

Ben heard the snark in Dale's tone. "You know I don't mean that."

"Don't you?"

"No, I don't, and I never once thought you'd be liable to steal." Ben bit down on his lip before he continued. "One of the programmes we have running on the estate is employing people from all backgrounds, who struggled to find work, including people newly released from prison. They come here to learn a trade, whether it's in the house or the gardens."

"And you trust them with your precious things?"

"Yes."

"But you have security guards?" Dale pointed out.

"I trust the people who come to work here. In the five years we've been running Calminster Moving On, I've only been let down twice."

Dale nodded contemplatively, as if Ben had given him food for thought. "I know a few kids who could have done with something like this. They ended up back in prison again because they couldn't find long-term work."

Ben pulled a face. "Unfortunately that's the one thing I can't offer them. This programme only lasts for a year after prison, but most of the people I help go on to find work, even if it's not exactly what they want. They get a good reference from me, and that really helps."

"You're a good man, Ben."

Ben flushed at Dale's obvious praise. "I've had a lot of privilege growing up. It would be wrong of me not to offer something back."

"Are we near one of those dark corners you mentioned?" Dale asked.

Ben was taken aback by the sudden change in subject. "Not too far away. Why?"

"I think I'd like to show you just how pleased I am that you are a decent man." Dale's voice was certainly hoarse and needy.

Shivering in anticipation, Ben drew Dale into one of the small bedrooms and then through into an even smaller room, which he informed Dale had been the valet's bedroom. "No one will find us here," he said.

Before Ben had drawn the next breath, Dale's mouth was on his, and thoughts and words became irrelevant.

Chapter Seven

DALE had been really offended with Ben's remark about his council house upbringing. He wasn't ashamed of his background, and he loved his mum to pieces, but in the face of so much wealth and privilege, he was feeling a little inadequate. And then in the next breath he'd felt ashamed at being annoyed with Ben, as Ben tried to explain about his plans to assist ex-cons back to employment. The only way Dale could think of getting over the awkward moment was to find a quiet corner and get on with the kissing.

His mouth on Ben's, his hands resting on Ben's hips gently—or maybe not so gently—shoving him against the wall, all this was to calm Dale's anger. Instead it transcended into something completely different. The spark that had been between them every time they stared into each other's eyes finally ignited into a white-hot flame. He hadn't intended to do anything more than a few chaste kisses today. Dale wanted to seduce Ben, a slow gentle process that Ben couldn't come back from, but his plans went up in ashes at the first touch of their mouths. Ben's lips parted under Dale's, and Dale took the opportunity to explore his mouth. Ben tasted of tea and the faintest sweetness from the earlier cakes.

Ben remained passive for a brief moment, as if he wasn't sure what to do, but Dale didn't want passive. He wanted Ben to need this as much as he did. Dale cupped Ben's arse and dragged him up against his body. Ben groaned into Dale's mouth, and then he clutched at Dale's hair and dragged him down to kiss just as forcefully as Dale was kissing him.

Dale's brain reminded him that slow and chaste was the plan. Dale put his brain on hold with ABBA's greatest hits and said he would get back to it later. The rest of his body focused on the man in his arms. As Dale kissed him, Ben made sounds that Dale absorbed. It was an incredible turn-on, and Dale was as hard as a rock. He could feel Ben's arousal and thrilled to the fact Ben was as aroused as him. Ben's hands tangled in his hair, a slight bite of pain that just added to the sensation while Dale drowned in Ben's male smell, and the rasp of his stubble on Dale's cheeks.

He could have stood there, in a quiet dark corner, kissing Ben until they both came, but in the end they were thwarted by something as simple as a phone call. Dale raised his head reluctantly as he felt the vibration from one of Ben's pockets.

"Is that your phone, or is your dildo pleased to see me?" Okay, it was a bad joke, but Ben laughed and his eyes focused again.

Ben dug out his phone. "Dinner is ready."

Dale raised an eyebrow. "Do they always ring you to let you know dinner is ready?"

"They text," Ben corrected. "And yes, if they can't find me, they text me. Calminster is a big place, and I could be anywhere on the estate."

Dale frowned, his mind immediately moving to the idea of Ben bringing other men to hide and play. Ben slipped his hand under Dale's T-shirt and pinched the skin on Dale's waist.

Dale yelped and scowled at him. "What did you do that for?"

"You're being an idiot," Ben said bluntly. "Yes, I've brought other men here, and no, none of them meant anything."

"Does that mean I'm special?"

"You're certainly something," Ben agreed.

Dale wanted to take exception to Ben's sarcastic reply, but Ben had taken the opportunity to give him a thorough grope. Dale decided his time would be better spent enjoying the fondle, and he could bitch later. Ben stepped back with a satisfied hum. Before he could say anything, Dale heard another vibration.

"Time to go?" Dale asked.

"They'll come hunting for me soon."

"We can't have them discovering you fondling the hired help."

Ben frowned. "You're not the hired help."

Dale opened his mouth and then shut it again. He'd meant it as a joke but realized it could have been taken a different way. He was quickly learning that they would have to tread carefully around the difference in their status.

"If you feed me, you can call me whatever you like."

"I think I can do that," Ben said.

THEY emerged from the small bedroom seconds before Colson ran up the stairs and spotted them. Dale was sure their appearances gave away exactly what they had been doing, but Colson was professional enough not to comment beyond saying that dinner had been served. Ben thanked him and led Dale to a large room he'd not been in before. He had already told Dale that they wouldn't eat in the dining room because it was being refurbished.

Dale blinked at the volume of food laid out on the table. "How many people are coming to dinner?"

Ben laughed and pointed Dale to a seat. "This is just for you and me. Mrs. Wilson was so thrilled to have her rescuer to dinner, she insisted on giving Lisa the menu. I usually eat in the kitchen unless I have guests. Don't worry, most of this food will reappear as leftovers over the next few days."

Dale was pleased when Ben took the seat next to him rather than at one end of the table. "I don't mind eating in the kitchen next time."

Ben's mouth quirked at one corner. "You think there's going to be a next time?"

"I thought we'd had this discussion already." Dale was sure there would be more than one next time. He didn't know where he got this confidence from, but he knew he and Ben were good for more than one dinner and a few kisses.

Or maybe not. Ben didn't answer immediately, and Dale started to worry he'd jumped the gun.

"I think there's going to be a next time," Ben agreed.

They served themselves rather than waiting for Colson to come back. Dale really hoped Ben didn't have some ritual about grace before dinner. He could remember going to Baz's father's house and being scowled at because he went to eat before Mr. Bromley had said grace. But Ben started eating almost before his arse hit the chair. Dale moaned at the first taste of Mrs. Wilson's chicken and vegetable pie. This wasn't haute cuisine. It was plain ordinary English cooking, like Dale's mother would serve him, but five hundred times better. Ben laughed when Dale told him this, around a mouthful of cheesy mashed potato that melted Dale's taste buds.

"I pay Mrs. Wilson a fortune never to retire."

"If I had your money, I'd do the same thing," Dale agreed.

"I went out to dinner last night, and although the food was good, I raided the freezer as soon as I got back, because nothing beats Mrs. Wilson's cooking."

"Who did you go out with?"

Ben seemed to brace himself before he answered. "There's something I ought to tell you before you read it in the gossip column."

"I don't read gossip columns," Dale pointed out.

"If you don't read it, then someone is bound to tell you."

"Go on, then."

Ben couldn't miss the edge to Dale's voice. "Until last night I was going out with a woman."

Dale felt as if Ben had delivered a punch to his gut. He sucked in a breath and said calmly as could, "Does this mean you separated from her?"

"I told you that I'm faithful to my boyfriends," Ben reminded him. "And I was faithful to Sabrina. We just didn't have a physical relationship."

"You used her for business?" Dale stiffened. He had been down this route before and wasn't about to see another woman used for convenience.

"I thought I could manage a platonic relationship with Sabrina, but I realized recently that she and her father were expecting more from me than just taking her out for the occasional date. Sabrina wanted to take things into the bedroom, and her father was expecting me to give her a ring. And I don't mean using the phone." Ben leaned back in his chair and sighed. "I knew I had to break things off with her."

"Because you didn't want that," Dale said.

Ben shook his head. "Going out with Sabrina was lazy and convenient, but it was wrong of me to lead her along. Although I might have ended up marrying her, because I'm a coward."

Dale frowned. "But you're gay."

"I'm also someone who is expected to marry and produce heirs."

"So what stopped you?"

Dale's heart faltered when Ben leaned over and took his hand. "I met you."

"Me?" Dale thought he knew what Ben meant, but he wanted him to say it out loud so they didn't have any misunderstandings between them.

"The minute I laid eyes on you, I wanted to...."

"To?"

Ben glared at him. "Do I really have to say this?"

Dale smirked. "Yes, you do."

"Dale Maloney, I wanted you to take me to bed and fuck me senseless."

Dale patted Ben's hand. "There, it wasn't so hard to say, was it?"

"You're a dick," Ben snapped.

"True," Dale agreed. "But I needed to know what you want from me. Thanks for ending things with Sabrina before you started things with me."

"I don't know that I want to now," Ben sniped, but he nodded as well. "Honestly, I am always faithful to my partners. I know I'm old-fashioned, but I don't really care."

"You have integrity," Dale said. "I like that. I'm old-fashioned too."

"And the idea of taking me to bed?"

Their hands were still joined, a connection they both needed. "I can do that. But are you prepared to wait awhile? It's still been only a few weeks since I split up from Baz, and I am still raw about that."

Ben picked up Dale's hand and brushed his knuckles with his lips. "We can take as long as you want."

"It won't be that long," Dale promised.

"As long as you want." Ben seemed determined to reassure Dale, which Dale found amusing as he was usually the one leading the situation.

"How did Sabrina take the news?" Dale asked.

Ben huffed out a breath. "She was amazing. I thought at first we were going to have a blazing row in the middle of the restaurant, but by the end of it, I had employed her new firm of lawyers to take care of my business."

Dale blinked as he thought about it. "How did that happen?"

"I have no idea, although I think I'm going to have to be really wary of Sabrina. Her father is a shark, but I have a feeling Sabrina is going to be even worse."

"If she is your lawyer, isn't she meant to be on your side?"

Ben shrugged and gave a short laugh. "In theory. Watch this space."

Dale was tired of talking about Sabrina. He started eating again, although he was still holding on to Ben's hand and using his fork with the other. It was complicated, but he could manage it. Ben didn't seem to object, and they finished their dinner in companionable silence.

As they were drinking coffee, Dale glanced at his watch. "I can't be too late tonight. I've got an early start tomorrow."

"How are you getting on at the fire station?"

"If you'd asked me that before I took down the maypole, I'm sure my answer would have been different," Dale said ruefully. "I don't think they're ever going to let me forget it. I now have fifteen L-plates sitting in Bertha."

Ben's lips twitched, but he delicately said nothing.

They finished the coffee, and Ben walked Dale to the huge wooden front doors.

"I'm glad you came," Ben said.

Dale leaned in and brushed Ben's ear with his mouth. "Next time I actually might." He chuckled as Ben flushed. "Good night, your lordship."

"I look forward to it. Night, Dale."

Chapter Eight

BEN watched Dale vanish into the darkness with a great deal of regret but also some relief. As much as he wanted to get Dale into his bed, Ben knew he had a great deal to sort out, and maybe some space wasn't a bad idea. He closed the veranda doors and locked each one before he switched out the light and left the study.

Colson emerged from the dining room to meet him. "Is there anything I can get you and Mr. Maloney, Mr. Ben?"

"Dale has gone home. I think I'll go to bed now." Ben noticed the surprise on Colson's face. "Whatever it is, spit it out."

"I thought Mr. Maloney would be staying the night," Colson said.

"Dale has an early start tomorrow. Go home, Colson. I'll see you in the morning."

"Good night, Mr. Ben." Colson bowed his head and then vanished toward the kitchen. He technically lived in a cottage on the estate, but quite often he slept at Calminster Hall, if he was too tired to go home. Ben didn't mind who slept at the Hall if a senior member of staff knew they were there.

Ben wandered up the stairs. He gave a massive yawn and rubbed his eyes. It had been a long day, and he needed to sleep. His bedroom took up a large part of the east wing. It was more like a suite, with large bedroom, en suite bathroom, and a walk-in closet. Once upon a time, this had been the nursery area, and his parents slept in the west wing. When Ben had inherited the Hall, he decided to keep his bedroom where it was and make two smaller bedrooms out of his suite. He left his parents' room, which was the master bedroom, as part of the guided tour they did during the summer season.

Ben collapsed onto the bed and thought about the evening he'd just had. It was ironic that he'd fallen for a fireman, considering the explosive chemistry between them. He knew even if nothing happened, he'd made the right decision about Sabrina. His physical reaction to Dale was a hundred times more than he felt for her. Wearily, Ben got to his feet, stripped off, and padded into the bathroom. He cleaned his teeth and then came back into the bedroom to fall face-first onto his bed. He wondered what Dale was doing at this precise moment. Probably stumbling through the trees. Perhaps Ben ought to have offered him a lift home. A smile curved his lips. He wanted to offer Dale a ride, but it didn't involve a car. He breathed out as all parts of his body registered its interest at riding Dale.

"Next time," Ben said into the darkness, "Next time, my fireman."

THREE days later Ben was working when he heard raised voices outside his study. One of them was definitely Colson, but he didn't recognize the other voice. He frowned, not pleased at being disturbed, and was about to find out what was going on when the study door burst open.

"You can't go in there, Mr. Barrett." Colson made an attempt to bar the way, but the man shoved him to one side. "I'm sorry, your lordship."

Fluffy and Fern growled, and Frankie snarled and yipped, but Barrett ignored them.

"It's okay, Colson." Ben attempted a smile at his unwanted visitor. "Thomas, this is unexpected." Maybe that was stretching it a little. He'd been expecting this confrontation since his meeting with Sabrina.

Thomas Barrett, Sabrina's father, scowled at Ben. "What the hell do you think you're playing at, Calminster?" Barrett was as immaculately dressed as ever. Sabrina got her style and her sharklike temperament from her father.

Ben ignored his outburst and looked at Colson. "Please, could you bring in coffee and take the dogs with you?"

"Yes, your lordship." Colson withdrew with an icy glare at Barrett, ushering the dogs out of the room. The three animals slunk out, clearly unhappy at being separated from their master in the face of potential danger.

"Take a seat," Ben said, settling himself in one of the armchairs.

Barrett stalked over to the other armchair and sat down. "You've got some explaining to do, Calminster."

"Sabrina told you that we're no longer seeing each other?" Ben said as calmly as he could.

"You haven't split up." Thomas jabbed his finger at Ben, his face ruddy with rage. "You'll marry my daughter."

Ben stared at him. "With all due respect, Barrett, my previous relationship with Sabrina is not your business, and my name is *Lord Calminster*." Ben spent his whole life playing down his title, but not today. Barrett needed to be reminded who he was dealing with. Lord Muckety-Muck indeed.

Barrett ignored the warning signal. "Of course it's my business. She's my daughter, and she'll do as she's told. You will marry her, and Barrett and Barrett will take over the Calminster estate as part of Calminster Enterprises."

"You seem to be laboring under a misapprehension. I've never had any intention of letting your company take over the Calminster estate. It was never part of the deal, and I'm certainly not marrying your daughter."

"Yes, you bloody well are. Calminster Hall is going to be the flagship hotel of Barrett Media and Leisure. Our wedding will be the society wedding of the decade."

Our wedding? Ben gritted his teeth and restrained the urge to smack the living daylights out of his guest. Barrett had ambitions that stretched beyond business. He wanted to get into society and saw Ben and Calminster as his access to a status that, thus far, had been out of his reach. All the Barrett money hadn't been able to break the class barrier; Ben was the means to change that.

"I'm sorry, Thomas, but Sabrina and I have come to an understanding—"

Barrett sprung to his feet. "If you think I'm going let you walk away after all the time and money I've spent organizing this merger, you're very mistaken, Calminster. I don't care if you're a poof, you're doing what you're fucking told to do."

"I think you ought to leave now, Barrett." Ben stood as well, unwilling to let the man dominate him.

"You will marry my daughter!" Barrett spat, clenching his fists.

Sure Barrett was about to take a swing, Ben prepared himself to tackle him. Although Barrett was taller and broader than him, Ben was fitter and ready to knock the bastard out if necessary. But before either one of them could make a move, there was a knock at the door.

Ben kept his eyes on Barrett as he said, "Enter."

Colson opened the door, but instead of coffee, he ushered Dale in. He'd obviously warned Dale there was an issue, because Dale looked as if he was prepared for a fight, his eyes cold and his expression resolute.

"Mr. Barrett is just leaving, Colson."

"Certainly, your lordship," Colson said. "Mr. Barrett—?"

Barrett ignored Colson and turned on Ben. "This isn't over."

"Our business is finished," Ben said firmly. "Go home before I call the police and have you arrested for trespass."

"Security is on their way," Colson said.

Ben knew this was code for they were waiting outside the door and by the windows, and one yell would bring them in. Still, he wanted to keep things civilized. "Please just go home, Barrett. We can talk another day."

"You're finished, Calminster," Barrett blustered. "We had a deal. If you don't marry Sabrina, I'll make sure you regret it."

"Did you just threaten Lord Calminster?" Dale asked, speaking for the first time. "He told you to get the fuck out of here."

"Who the hell are you? Are you the fag boyfriend? I don't care if he's fucking you as long as he marries Sabrina and gets her knocked up."

Ben saw the fury on Dale's face. Barrett couldn't have said anything guaranteed to make Dale angrier. In the short time he'd known Dale, Ben had come to understand how raw Dale had been left by his ex's cheating with a woman. The last thing he needed was for Thomas Barrett to realize he'd struck a nerve.

"Get out, Barrett."

Dale took a step toward Barrett, who seemed to realize he was out-firemanned as he flinched back. As tall as Barrett was, Dale was a good few inches taller and twice his bulk, and with that expression on his face he was fucking menacing—and yes, Ben did thrill to Dale's caveman act.

Still, Barrett had to have the final word. "You haven't heard the last of this, Calminster."

Dale loomed again, and Barrett took a step backward; then, thankfully, he left, Colson at his back. Through the door, Ben could see the security men flanking Barrett.

That left him and Dale in the room alone. Ben dragged in a shaky breath. "Well, that was new."

Dale's jaw was clenched tight and his hands balled into fists. "Can he do you damage?"

"Possibly." As Dale narrowed his eyes, Ben shrugged. "If Barrett meddles in the boardroom, he could cause me serious problems. I'll need to talk to Sabrina."

"Do it now," Dale said. "I can wait."

Ben nodded, then tilted his head. "Kiss me first?"

Dale seemed to understand it was a plea, not a demand, and he stepped into Ben's space. He laid a large, warm hand on Ben's jaw and kissed him. The kiss started gently, but Ben didn't need tender; he needed hard and demanding to release the tension of frustration and anger in him. Ben made a noise in the back of his throat and pressed up against Dale, who tangled one hand in Ben's hair and the other on his arse, holding Ben firmly where he wanted him. Their tongues entwined and explored, a slight taste of mint in Dale's mouth. Ben reveled in being held tightly, never wanting to be let go. He rubbed up against Dale's body, feeling an answering bulge pressing against his stomach.

A polite cough interrupted him. "Your lordship?"

"Yes?" Ben snapped, keeping a soothing hand on Dale because judging from the thunderous expression on Dale's face, he was ready to snap Colson like a twig for disturbing them.

"Ms. Barrett's on the phone. I thought you might want to talk to her."

Ben huffed and ran a hand through his hair. "Yes, thank you. Do you mind?"

"You need to talk to her," Dale said, although he seemed to make an effort not to snap.

"I'll bring more coffee," Colson said and beat a hasty retreat.

"I'm sorry." Ben picked up the phone on his desk.

"You'd better make it up to me later." Dale slumped into an armchair.

"I will, I promise." Ben pressed the button. "Sabrina. Just the person I want to talk to."

"So how angry was my father when your fireman threw him out?"

"How do you…? He didn't…." Sabrina chuckled, and Ben realized she'd been winding him up. "Ha-ha, very funny."

"I wish I'd been there."

"Your father's going to cause trouble with the other board members."

"I know," she said calmly. "I'm ready for him."

Ben felt some of his tension ease at her calmness. He didn't know if she was as good as she said she was, but he was prepared to trust her. "Make sure you talk to Freely. He's the biggest shareholder apart from your father. If anyone's going to support him, it'll be Freely."

"Relax, Ben. I can handle my father."

"Thanks, Sabrina." Ben smiled at Dale, who grinned back. He seemed more relaxed now.

Colson knocked once and came in with a tray of coffee and the dogs. Frankie jumped up on Dale's lap. Ben was pleased to see Dale didn't mind at all.

"I've got to go, Sabrina."

"Go and play with your boy," Sabrina said. "I'll go put out the fires my father's bound to start."

Ben disconnected the call and joined Colson and Dale. "Sabrina is on the case."

"You have the best ex ever." Dale slurped his coffee.

"She is pretty good. Thank you, Colson." Ben accepted his coffee. "Do you want to sit with us?"

Colson shook his head. "Mrs. Wilson is being discharged in a few days. I want to make sure the house is in order or she'll be fussing."

Once he left, Dale tangled his legs with Ben's. "How're you feeling?"

"I'm fine," Ben said, sighing.

"You sure?"

Ben nodded. "Barrett's going to cause me problems, but it's business. I can deal with that. It's much better than marrying his daughter for a business deal."

"I can't believe you actually contemplated going through with it."

"Nor can I," Ben confessed. "It just seemed easier."

"Easier than what?" Dale asked.

"Finding a man willing to put up with me."

Dale gave him a pseudo smile. "You mean it's easier to do the white wedding, having kids, and perpetuating the family name with a woman."

Ben immediately felt guilty, because of course that's what he meant. "I'm expected to produce an heir."

"Who's your heir if you don't have kids?"

"I've got a really nice cousin who lives in Australia. He'd be horrified if he inherited."

"We can have kids," Dale said.

Ben raised an eyebrow. "Isn't that a bit premature? Anyway, the last time I checked, two dicks don't make a baby."

"What about adoption or surrogacy?"

"It just seems so…." Ben struggled to find the right word.

"Complicated?" Dale suggested.

"Complicated."

"Is it worth it, though? You can be miserable with a woman or happy with a man. Or I guess there's a third option."

Ben frowned. "A third option?"

"Like Barrett said, you can marry a woman and have a man on the side."

"But not you."

Dale shook his head. "Not me." His expression was bleak but resolute. "I don't cheat—ever."

Ben nodded once. He understood what Dale was trying to tell him. He could have Dale as his partner, but only if he was prepared to be open and honest about it.

"My sister offered to be my surrogate," Dale said.

"Now?"

Dale chuckled. "I'm not talking right this second, but she and her husband offered if I ever found the right man—who wasn't Baz. She hated him."

"You mean I have to get the sister seal of approval?"

"Hell yes. She's a nightmare."

"Thanks for the warning," Ben said drily.

"At least I gave you the warning. I could have let you meet her cold. Baz calls her the Pit Bull."

Ben gave him an unfriendly stare. "I like pit bulls."

"I like my sister."

"I don't think I'd like Baz." Then Ben held his breath.

"He's an arsehole," Dale agreed. "Have we finished discussing my sister and ex-boyfriend now?"

"I think so. What do you want to do?"

Dale very deliberately put down his mug and held out his hand. Ben sat on the footstool beside Dale's chair. Dale tilted his head as if he was considering how to kiss Ben; then he placed his mouth on Ben's. The kiss started tender, and then, as before, the kiss got a little frantic.

Ben barely noticed Frankie, who jumped off Dale's lap in disgust and stalked away to his usual sleeping place under the desk.

The chemistry between Ben and Dale was incendiary, their hands all over each other clutching and pulling, until they were virtually humping each other.

Dale pulled back, gasping for air. Ben stayed where he was, sprawled over him. "Christ, I was planning a slow, quiet seduction."

"You managed the seduction, but there's nothing slow or quiet." Instead he felt like they were an armful of dynamite just ready to explode. He had to kiss Dale again, licking out the taste of coffee and need.

Ben frowned as Dale lifted Ben off him and sat him back on the footstool. "What's wrong?"

"We need to slow down." Dale took a few deep breaths and put some space between them.

"Slow down? Why?" Ben knew he sounded incredulous and more than a shade whiny. Dale ran his hands through his hair. Ben wanted to smooth it down, but his body was still thrumming with arousal, while his head was struggling with Dale's rejection.

Dale sat so Ben's knees were between his, and he held Ben's hands. "You're really something, my Lord Calminster."

"A good something or a bad something?"

"You're amazing." Dale's smile was a little shaky, but Ben could see his sincerity.

Ben stroked his thumb over Dale's wrist. "Why did you stop?"

"Because…." Dale shook his head. "A few weeks ago, I found my boyfriend screwing a woman in my bed on the day I intended to propose, and now you're here and—"

"And you're feeling vulnerable?" Ben nodded at Dale's press of his lips. "It's okay. I can wait for you to be ready."

Dale's hands tightened on his. "Are you sure?"

"I'm sure, although maybe we ought to keep our hands off each other." Ben smirked wickedly at Dale. "Do you think you can do that?"

"I don't know. You're kind of addictive." Dale looked a bit sheepish.

They both chuckled, and then Frankie jumped on Dale's lap.

"You can't have him," Ben chided the small dog and went to push him on the floor, but Frankie yipped and settled down on Dale's lap, encouraging Dale to pat him gently.

Ben huffed and flung himself into one of the armchairs across from Dale. From the triumphant expression on Frankie's face, he obviously realized he'd won that round.

"You won the battle, but you're not winning the war," Ben informed the dog.

Dale scritched behind Frankie's ears and Frankie closed his eyes, ignoring his frustrated owner.

Chapter Nine

DALE drove along the driveway to Calminster Hall as fast as he could, anxious to see Ben after four days on shift. It had been frustrating not to see him over the past few days, knowing he was just a couple of miles away. Dale had spent the time working, running, and sleeping, but he managed FaceTime with Ben every day, although it wasn't as good as face-to-face.

As he pulled up, he spotted Ben on the stone steps with two men, a fixed smile on his face and his body language screaming out for rescue. Dale was just the man for the job. As he approached them, Dale saw one of the men lean into Ben's space and wag his finger. It was all he could do not to wrench the man away from Ben.

"Just because you've got some fancy title doesn't give you the right to throw me out of my house."

Before Dale could intervene, Ben drew himself up and said, in a voice dripping with ice, "I own the house, Miller, and the job that you never turned up to. You think because you've lived in the house all your life that you can do whatever you like? I run a business, not a holiday home."

"The old lord didn't have a problem."

"I'm not my father."

"That's bloody obvious, you pompous self-entitled po—"

"For God's sake, Chaz, shut up." The other man, who so far had just stood to one side looking embarrassed, finally intervened. "His lordship's got a point. You're never at work, and when you are, you're always drunk."

Miller turned on his friend so fast he swayed, and Dale realized he was probably drunk now. "You bastard!"

Before he could get any further, Ben said, "Go home, Miller. Getting arrested won't help you find work or a new home. We'll talk on Monday. Take him away before he makes an even bigger fool of himself."

Chaz dragged his friend, who was still screaming slurred insults and making threats, past Dale.

When they finally disappeared into a battered old Fiesta and drove away, Ben gave Dale a weak grin. "You heard all that?"

Dale nodded. "You handled it well."

"I've got experience," Ben said wryly.

"I nearly thumped him."

"Thanks for not intervening," Ben said. "I need to handle Miller myself. He already thinks I'm weak."

"He doesn't know you at all."

Ben tilted his head. "And you do?"

"Yeah," Dale said. "I *know* you." He watched the color fill Ben's face and smiled with smug satisfaction.

Rather than say anything, Ben took the steps and opened the front door. Immediately, the three dogs rushed out to greet them. Dale patted and stroked them, assuring them all they were the best dogs in the world. Ben beamed at him for loving on his furry family and drew him into his arms for a quick kiss. Dale growled low in his throat, because he wanted more than a chaste kiss.

Ben placed a finger over Dale's lips. "Come see Mrs. Wilson. She is anxious to thank you."

"She got discharged today?"

"They couldn't keep her in." Ben gave a fond smile. "I swear that woman is made of Calminster stone."

"She's amazing," Dale said. "I tell you, my heart plummeted when I saw her in the garden."

"She doesn't even remember the fire or the garden. Just making the toast and worrying about the cat."

"What did happen to the cat?"

"Her neighbor's got Sparkles for now. We'd have brought her here, but Frankie doesn't play well with cats."

Dale smirked. "Aren't most cats twice the size of Frankie?"

Ben scowled at him. "Shhh, he doesn't know that. He has a big-dog complex."

"He don't take no shit from anyone," Dale agreed. "How is Mrs. Wilson?"

Ben sobered a little. "I think she's still in shock. The full comprehension of what's happened hasn't really hit her yet. Sandra wants to take her back home with her, but Mrs. Wilson is determined to get back to work. She's staying here at the Hall for a few days while we get a new cottage ready for her, and then we'll play it by ear."

"Come and take me to Mrs. Wilson," Dale said, "and then I think you promised me dinner?"

Ben gave him a quick kiss and guided him to a room Dale had only seen in passing. There, Dale found what felt like most of the village gathered around Mrs. Wilson, who was sitting in a large armchair. She appeared—Dale sought a word—*fragile*. As if the trauma of the fire had knocked a large hole in her psyche. To Dale's mind, the shock was just beginning to hit her. Mrs. Wilson smiled as she caught sight of Dale and held out her hand. Dale took her chilled, wrinkled hand in his and rubbed it gently. Then he got down to her level and asked her how she was feeling.

"I feel just fine," Mrs. Wilson assured him. She must have caught sight of his skeptical expression, because she said, "The doctors say my lungs are fine, and I wasn't burned. I just feel such a ninny for tripping over the cat."

"That bloody cat is a menace." The woman who spoke sat next to Mrs. Wilson and looked like a younger version of her, so Dale assumed this was Sandra.

Mrs. Wilson made a tutting noise. "Sparkles is a lovely cat." From the various snorts, Dale gathered Mrs. Wilson was the only one who thought so, but Mrs. Wilson blithely ignored them all and addressed her remarks to Dale. "I think someone was taking care of me that day. You were guided to find me."

Dale had attended many fires, and most of the time, he didn't see the aftermath and the effect on the people who had lost their world. Mrs. Wilson was indeed a remarkable woman to see such a positive outcome.

"I think so too. I was so relieved to find you safe and sound."

She patted his hand. "Mr. Ben said he promised you dinner."

"I've heard so much about your cooking."

"I'm not really in the swing of things yet, but it will only take a couple of days, and Lisa's holding the fort." She grinned at her employer, who was a couple of steps away. "Take your young man away and feed him."

Dale stiffened, not sure how Ben was going to take that. But when he risked a glance at Ben's face, he realized Ben had missed it because he was talking to someone else.

Dale looked back at Mrs. Wilson. She stared at him calmly. "You know?"

"Of course I do," she said. "I've known since he was a child."

"You don't mind?"

"I only mind if you hurt him."

Dale squeezed her hand as gently as he could. "That's not going to happen."

Mrs. Wilson beamed at him again. "There's no worry, then. Mr. Ben…."

"I hope you've not been giving away all my secrets, Mrs. Wilson." Ben raised an eyebrow at her.

"Not yet," she said. "Go and eat before the dinner is overcooked."

"I'm in no rush." Dale's stomach rumbled, betraying him, making them all laugh.

"Come on," Ben said. "I need food as well. I've not eaten since breakfast."

"Oh, Mr. Ben." Mrs. Wilson sounded disappointed in him.

"I was busy. I'll make up for it now."

"What about Mrs. Wilson and your guests?" Dale asked.

"It's all been taken care of," Ben assured him. "Colson and Lisa have been working flat out all afternoon to make sure there is plenty of food for everyone."

Dale looked at him suspiciously. "I thought you were cooking for me?"

Ben shrugged. "It seems a little churlish to ignore their efforts, don't you think?"

From down below, Mrs. Wilson snorted. "Mr. Ben promised to cook for you? It'll be a cold day in hell before he uses a tin opener in my kitchen."

Ben rolled his eyes in frustration, but Dale just agreed with her. "He was going to take the credit for someone else's work."

"It's the way it always is," she said. "Never take anything he says for granted."

"You're going to put him off me," Ben protested.

Mrs. Wilson looked up at him with a gentle smile. "You just tell the truth to your young man and he'll see you for the big heart you are."

To Dale's amusement Ben blushed furiously and mumbled something about the ground opening up. Before Dale could drag Ben away, Sandra rushed over and flung her arms around Dale.

"Thank you. Thank you."

Dale hugged her and then stepped backward. "I'm just glad Mrs. Wilson is all right."

She knuckled at her eyes and smiled at him. "You make sure everyone knows how grateful we are."

"I'll tell them," Dale assured her.

Ben made his apologies and then led Dale away. He waited until they were outside the room with the door shut before he said, "I'll make sure your station commander knows how grateful we all are. If there is anything I can donate to the station, anything at all, you know I'll do it."

Dale looked at Ben. "We were just doing our job. You know that."

Ben lightly caressed Dale's hair. Dale mentally thanked God that he had washed his hair before he came out, because it had been covered in soot and ash from a skip fire. "You're doing an amazing job, Dale."

Dale squirmed in embarrassment. "I thought you were going to feed me."

Ben just laughed and led him to the kitchen. The dogs joined them as they sat down. "I'm sure we can find you a sausage roll or two."

"Huh, I was expecting proper food. I'm not sure I'm hungry now." Dale's stomach growled loudly again. "Traitor!"

Ben went to the range and pulled out a tray of roasted meat and vegetables. "I hope you like lamb."

"I love it," Dale said fervently, salivating over the aroma.

Ben dished out the food and came to the table with two large plates of roast lamb, potatoes, and vegetables. Then he went back to the range and pulled out a jug, which he brought to the table. Dale saw it was gravy. As he went to touch it, Ben smacked his hand.

"Don't do that," Ben scolded. "The jug will be hot." Using a cloth, Ben covered Dale's food in gravy and then his own.

Dale politely waited for Ben to sit down; then he tucked in, moaning around the first mouthful.

Ben raised an eyebrow. "You like your food, don't you?"

"I'm a big man, and there's a lot to fill. I love food," Dale admitted. "Any food. I am not fussy. We'll cook at the fire station. Once you've eaten and survived half-cooked-chicken food poisoning, you can just about eat anything."

"I think you're safe with me," Ben said.

Dale showed his appreciation by eating every scrap of food on the plate, to the disappointment of Frankie, Fluffy, and Fern. If he had been on his own, he'd probably have licked the plate clean too.

Even better, once Ben cleared away the plates, he produced a large slice of strawberry pavlova, made with fresh strawberries from the grounds. Dale ate his slice and then most of Ben's, as Ben assured him he wasn't hungry.

Finally, Dale sat back and rubbed his stomach. "That was amazing."

"You're welcome." Ben offered him the coffeepot, and Dale said yes. "We'll grab our coffees and go and sit in my study. Unless you want to go back and sit with everybody else?"

Dale shook his head. "I'm quite tired, and there were a lot of people there. Some quiet time with you is just what I need." He quailed at the thought of facing that crowd again and took heart in the shy smile Ben gave him.

They didn't meet anyone as they crossed the hall to Ben's private study, although they could hear laughter coming from the room with the villagers. Ben shut the door of the study, and in the silence Dale felt nervous. He took a seat on the sofa and hoped the smile he gave Ben was confident. From the uncertain look on Ben's face, it seemed Ben was feeling the same as he was. They drank their coffee for a few minutes, and then Ben put the mug down on what Dale thought was probably a priceless antique and turned to Dale.

"Are you working tomorrow?"

"Yes, but I'm on two nights."

Ben pulled a face. "I'm going to have to get used to your shift patterns."

"I'll give you a copy," Dale promised.

"Stay here the night," Ben said. "You don't have to get up in the morning, and I don't have to rush. Stay the night with me. We don't have to do anything except sleep." The last words were rushed, as if he was worried about Dale's response.

Dale trailed his fingers down Ben's cheekbones and jaw. "I'd like that, but what about the rest of the staff?"

"They're going to have to get used to seeing you here."

"Are you sure you're ready for that?" Dale asked.

Ben frowned. "You sound worried. Are you expecting trouble? Has anyone said anything to you?"

"Everyone has been really supportive. I guess it's just years of living with Baz. I'm used to having to hide my relationships."

Ben nodded and put a little space between himself and Dale. "My staff work for me, and they protect my privacy. I've had men here before."

Dale was jealous of every man Ben had kissed, but he wasn't stupid enough to make an issue of it. This time Ben wanted to take him to bed. Dale was confident he could put every other man out of Ben's mind. He had mad skills and was determined to show Ben every single one.

If Ben was aware of Dale's sudden attack of green eyes, he chose to ignore it. Dale waited patiently as Ben spent a few minutes saying good night to people as they gradually left. Sandra had already taken her mother to her bedroom and agreed to spend the night there, just in case her mother needed her.

"I'm going to spend the night here too, Mr. Ben," Colson said. "Just in case Mrs. Wilson needs any medical attention."

Ben said good night to those who were left and led Dale away.

"You have very devoted staff," Dale said as they walked up the stairs.

"They're the closest thing I've got to a family. Colson would rather sleep on the kitchen floor than abandon his post. Does that seem feudal to you?"

"It's different," Dale admitted, "but it's nice to know you have people who care for you."

Dale was aware of the sudden tension in Ben as he shut the door to his bedroom. He knew Ben had brought men here, but Ben was nervous about Dale. He wasn't sure if that was good or bad.

Ben rubbed his eyes.

"You look exhausted," Dale said.

"So do you." They looked at each other, and then Ben chuckled. "Let's sleep, and we can take this further in the morning. If I stand here any longer, I'll fall asleep with my eyes open. There's fresh toothbrushes in the cabinet in the bathroom. You go in there first."

By the time Ben had used the bathroom, Dale was settled in bed on the left side, still wearing his T-shirt and briefs. "I wasn't sure what side you sleep on, but I guessed it must be the right side."

As the bedside table on the right side had a clock and a book, it wasn't exactly rocket science, but Ben didn't call him out on it. Instead he settled into bed and turned out the light. Immediately Dale wrapped himself around Ben, reveling in the feel of Ben in his arms.

"I'm not always going to be the little spoon," Ben said in the darkness.

Dale yawned and then pressed a kiss in the nape of Ben's neck. "Good night."

"I mean it."

"Later," Dale said. "I'm too tired to argue now."

Ben huffed, but he settled down in Dale's arms, and soon enough his breathing eased into sleep. Dale took a while longer, but he didn't care. He was happy where he was.

Chapter Ten

BEN shivered as he woke, fumbling to find the cover without opening his eyes. It was only when the duvet was nowhere to be found that he cranked open one eye and found the reason he was cold. Dale had somehow managed to steal Ben's side of the duvet and wrap it around himself. He was fast asleep and happily warm and snug.

Unlike Ben.

"Give me back the duvet!" Ben tugged futilely on one corner. Dale was wrapped tighter than a Russian baby all swaddled up. Dale grumbled as Ben disturbed him, but he didn't wake up, and he hung on even tighter, which enraged Ben. "I'm cold. Give me the bloody duvet!"

He tugged and pulled until eventually Dale let go enough that Ben could cover himself again. Ben sighed with pleasure as the warmth surrounded him. Then Dale rolled and wrapped himself around Ben, who contemplated throwing him off, but Dale was like a furry hot water bottle. Ben hadn't really noticed the body hair last night. He opened his eyes and frowned. Last night Dale had been clothed. Now… Ben was damn sure it wasn't a pair of briefs poking his arse.

"Morning," Dale mumbled and nuzzled Ben's neck. "Feeling warmer?"

"No thanks to you." Ben pushed back against Dale's warmth, still somewhat cold.

"Yeah, I should have warned you, I have a habit of stealing the covers." Dale sounded more smug than sorry. He wrapped his arms around Ben and held him tight.

"Don't do it again," Ben mumbled, his irritation fading as he warmed.

"No promises." Dale wriggled against Ben. "I'm awake now."

"I can see that," Ben said. "And naked."

"You're awake."

"Yes?" Ben kept the amusement out of his voice.

"And not naked."

"I'm cold."

"Maybe I could warm you up a little?" Dale sounded hopeful.

"I'm just fine now."

"You don't want playtime before we get up?" Dale raised up on one elbow and nibbled at Ben's shoulder.

"We can get breakfast if you're hungry, Dale," Ben pointed out.

"Or I could eat you."

Ben's dick twitched hopefully, fully on board with Dale's suggestion. *What the hell? It sounds like an awesome idea.* He rolled onto his back and wriggled out of his clothes. Then he stretched, ensuring Dale got a full look at his body.

"Go for it." Ben sucked in a deep breath and relaxed back against the sheets. This was what he'd missed when he was with Sabrina. This raw visceral male energy that made him feel alive. He closed his eyes and waited for....

"What the hell?" Dale's annoyed tone dragged Ben from the languorous reverie. Ben opened his eyes to see Dale glaring at the door.

"What's the matter?" Ben asked.

"Someone just knocked on the door and said breakfast is ready."

Ben blinked. He hadn't heard a thing.

The annoyance on Dale's face was replaced by amusement. "Didn't you hear them?"

Shaking his head, Ben struggled to sit up, only to be flattened again by Dale.

"Stay there," Dale growled.

"Breakfast—"

"Will have to wait!"

Ben grinned at Dale's aggrieved tone. He closed his eyes again. Breakfast could wait a few minutes. His silent consent obviously pleased Dale because he got back to business, licking a stripe up Ben's neck.

"For heaven's sake!"

"What now?" Ben whined.

"Your bloody butler is cockblocking me again. He's going to tip a bucket of water over us if we don't head downstairs."

"He said that?" Ben asked dubiously. Colson was the epitome of good manners.

"No, he just implied it with his knock."

Ben sat up with a huff. "You're too easily distracted."

Thunderclouds gathered across Dale's brow. "You text him and say we'll be down after we've fucked."

"If only I could." The moment was well and truly lost, and Ben swung his legs to the floor. "Next time, Dale."

Dale headed for the bathroom, his whole back radiating annoyance. Ben sighed. He was going to have to make it up to Dale later, but first he had to take Dale down to breakfast with the closest thing Ben had to family. God help the poor man.

MR. Colson, Mrs. Wilson, and Sandra sat around the scrubbed pine table, sharing a large pot of tea.

Mrs. Wilson took one look at them and sighed, shuffling over to the covered dishes on the large granite work surface. "What do you want to eat, Mr. Ben? Mr. Maloney?"

Ben would have been happy to make himself tea and toast, but he could see from the determination on her face that Mrs. Wilson wanted to be seen to do her duties. "Everything, please, Mrs. Wilson, and Dale will have the same."

Dale stiffened, but he just nodded. "Morning, Mrs. Wilson."

Ben shot a glance at Dale, begging him just to run with it. He'd apologize later for overriding him. Dale was still prickly about their interrupted lovemaking. For now they both had to make nice with Mrs. Wilson. Dale gave a brief nod as they sat down.

Sandra smirked at them, and Colson concentrated on his cup of tea.

"I was about to send Mr. Colson up again," Mrs. Wilson scolded as she set down the plates piled high with bacon, eggs, mushrooms, and hash browns in front of Ben and Dale.

"You'd have been better to turn the hose on them," Sandra said.

"Sandra!" Mrs. Wilson tutted, but Ben could see the grin she was trying to hide. She brought toast to the table, smacking Sandra's hand when she reached for a slice. "You've had yours. This is for his lordship and Mr. Maloney."

"What do I have to do to persuade you to call me Dale, Mrs. Wilson?" Dale asked. He sounded more relaxed than he had a few minutes previously.

She poured out a cup of tea before she answered. "Normally I don't address his lordship's friends by their given name." Ben was about to nudge Dale to ask him not to pursue it when Mrs. Wilson continued. "But you're one of us. So, *Dale*, would you like tea?"

"I would love a cup, please. Strong as you can make it." Dale looked delighted, and Ben breathed a sigh of relief. Sabrina had never treated Colson or Mrs. Wilson as anything except staff, and she'd never have asked them to call her by her first name.

Dale had done more to get in Calminster Hall's good books in a couple of days than Sabrina had the whole time they had been going out. Rescuing Mrs. Wilson had given him a head start. Although that wasn't strictly accurate, Ben thought, as he remembered Dale coming over the first day and talking to Tim. He was naturally friendly to everyone.

Ben finished his breakfast and sat back, studying Mrs. Wilson. It was clear from the way she stooped and her shaky hands that she was struggling, but Colson caught his eye and gave a quick shake of his head. Ben nodded to say he understood. Mrs. Wilson didn't want to be coddled or made to feel like an invalid, especially in front of her daughter and Dale. He would have a quiet word with her later.

"Mrs. Wilson, that was magnificent."

She beamed at Dale's high praise, but she had to add, "It was even better when it was freshly cooked."

Dale gave her an exaggerated wink. "I'll remember that for next time. May I help you clear up?"

She shook her head, but she was obviously pleased to be asked. "Nice to see Dale has manners, Mr. Ben, unlike some of your friends."

Ben rolled his eyes. She'd made her feelings plain about some of his former "friends" more than once. "If you're ready, Dale?"

"Ready for what?" Sandra asked, winking at him. "Seconds?"

"That's quite enough of that," Mrs. Wilson said primly.

Ben caught Dale's eye, and they vanished before they could be embarrassed again.

As they walked across the hall, Dale nudged Ben. "You didn't answer Sandra's question."

"Huh?"

"What am I ready for?"

Ben opened the door to his study and hustled Dale inside; then he slammed Dale up against the closed door. "This!"

Dale rested his hands on Ben's hips and raised an eyebrow. "Sandra was right, then? You want seconds? Although in our case, it'll still be firsts."

"Seconds and thirds." Ben kissed him, crushing Dale against the door. Dale didn't seem to mind, wrapping his arms around Ben, leaving no space between them. Eventually Ben pulled back for air, flushed, breathless, and ready to go again as soon as he'd quelled the burning in his lungs.

They stayed in the same position for long moments until Ben sighed and rested his head against Dale's shoulder. "I feel alive again."

Dale didn't pretend not to understand. "I don't know how you even thought you could be with a woman."

"I've got past the girls-have-cooties stage."

"Except teenage girls."

Ben's head snapped up. "How did you—? You've been talking to Mrs. Manning," Ben said with a touch of rancor.

"Maybe."

"She knows all my secrets."

"She does," Dale agreed.

"God bless her hairy chin. I know a few of hers."

Dale rubbed his chin against Ben's, stubble rasping on stubble. "But I'm not interested in Mrs. Manning's secrets. I'm only interested in you. I'm sorry I was in such a foul mood earlier."

"Next time," Ben promised, "there'll be no interruptions."

They didn't kiss, but they rested against each other, and Ben breathed in Dale's male scent. Dale didn't seem anxious to move or take things any further, so Ben stayed where he was, wrapped in Dale's arms.

Inevitably, they were disturbed before he was ready by a light tap at the door.

"Mr. Ben?" Lisa sounded almost tentative.

Ben sighed and stepped back, running his hands through his hair in an attempt to straighten up. Dale refused to let him go fully, instead keeping Ben close. "Yes?"

"Barry is here."

"Okay. I'll be with him in a moment."

"He's in the office."

Ben listened to her footsteps walk away. "I'm sorry, I know I said I'd clear my schedule, but I do need to talk to him. We're still trying to sort out suitable housing for Mrs. Wilson."

Dale kissed him before he spoke. "That's fine."

"Do you have to go home?"

"Not if you want me to stay."

Ben nodded. "This shouldn't take long."

Dale gathered Ben close and hugged him; then, almost reluctantly, Ben led Dale out of the room.

"Sorry to keep you waiting, Barry," Ben said as they entered the study.

"No worries, Mr. Ben," Barry said. "Mr. Maloney."

"Call me Dale." Dale shook hands with Barry. "I'm going to find Tim."

Ben was reluctant to let Dale out of his sight, but he nodded, and Dale vanished into the garden.

For the next thirty minutes, Ben and Barry discussed where they were going to rehouse Mrs. Wilson. For anybody else it would be an easy thing to do, but Mrs. Wilson was Mrs. Wilson, and she demanded, and was freely given, a better level of care. They had a number of empty cottages in the village as people moved away, but some of them had steep steps and others catered to larger families. Ben's great-grandfather, despite his profligate ways, had been a man with vision. And he had built the village to accommodate many types of residents, including those in their later years. When Ben's grandfather took over the baronetcy, he continued his father's vision to look after the residents of Calminster village.

Ben and Barry had managed to pin down three separate cottages they thought might suit Mrs. Wilson.

They went in search of her and discovered her making tea. She smiled at them when they entered the kitchen.

"Just in time for a cuppa," she said. "What can I do for you, gentlemen?"

"Barry and I found three cottages we think you might like. Do you have time to sit down and discuss it with us?" Ben asked.

Mrs. Wilson continued to pour the tea and offer them homemade shortbread as though she hadn't heard the question.

Sandra bit her lip, then said, "Mum, did you hear what Mr. Ben asked?"

"My hearing's just fine, thank you, Sandra," Mrs. Wilson said acerbically. "I was hoping to go back to my home."

There was a moment's silence where Ben, Barry, and Sandra all looked at each other, and then Sandra said, very gently as if she didn't want to spook her mother, "You haven't seen the place, Mum. It really needs demolishing and starting again. It would be months before you could move back there."

Mrs. Wilson's lips moved but she didn't say anything, and she seemed to stumble backward, her hand out behind her. Everyone moved in so she wouldn't fall over, but Barry got there first, steadying Mrs. Wilson and easing her down to the chair.

"I hoped you were going to tell me it could be repaired," Mrs. Wilson said brokenly. "Just like when the tank flooded. I only had to move out for a couple of weeks."

Ben sat down in the chair next to her and took Mrs. Wilson's hands. "When the tank flooded, it only damaged part of the house. Now the whole cottage has gone. It would be better for me to demolish the place and rebuild it." He felt her flinch as she processed what he'd said.

"Has my home really gone?"

"It's just a shell." Ben knew it was brutal, but he had to make her understand.

Mrs. Wilson's face crumpled and tears spilled onto her cheeks. "I only tripped over Sparkles and then burned the toast."

"I know, but the tea towel caught fire, and that spread to the rest of the kitchen."

"I'm so sorry, Mr. Ben."

"You have nothing to be sorry for. It was just an accident."

"What am I going to do? I've got nothing left."

"You've got us," Ben said. "And Sandra. And the village. We'll all take care of you, I promise."

Mrs. Wilson's face crumpled. "I could take care of myself in my own home."

"And you will again, Mum, once we find you and that damn cat somewhere nice to live." Sandra took her mother into her arms, and both men retreated to give them some space.

"We'll carry on with this later," Ben said.

Barry nodded and looked at his watch. "I've got a meeting with the gamekeeper."

"If you see Dale, tell him I'll be at the stables."

"Will do." Barry vanished, leaving Ben with the two women.

Mrs. Wilson wiped her eyes and noisily blew her nose. "I'd like to stay with Sandra for a few days."

"I think that's a good idea," Ben agreed.

"What about the kitchen?"

"You leave Mr. Ben to worry about that, Mum," Sandra said.

Ben nodded in agreement. "We'll all cope. You just concentrate on getting better."

Mrs. Wilson got to her feet with Sandra's help. It was plain to see how traumatized she was now the shock was wearing off. For the first time, Mrs. Wilson looked her age, and Ben wondered if she would be able to return to the Hall. Perhaps it was time he needed a replacement cook. He sighed as the door closed behind them. Another piece of his past coming to an end. Ben knew he didn't handle change all that well. Then Dale popped his head around the veranda doors and smiled at him. Ben smiled back, thinking maybe he could handle some change just fine.

Chapter Eleven

TEARS traced a path through the soot on Mr. Hamilton's cheeks. "I've got to go to her. She needs me."

"Let the paramedic treat you," Dale said. "I'll bring Bonnie here."

To Dale's relief, Mr. Hamilton stayed where he was, and the paramedic continued to wrap his hands in gauze as Dale went to Bertha. Mr. Hamilton had burns and scrapes from where he'd tried to rescue his friend from a burning shed. The fire crew had tried to save Bonnie by giving her oxygen, but it was too late, and now she rested on the grass, destined to hop no more.

This was just the latest of a long week of callouts, which they were beginning to suspect were the work of one person. None of the fires were more than garden sheds, skips, and rubbish bins, but today the fires claimed their first victim—Bonnie, a beautiful blue lop-eared rabbit who had been Mr. Hamilton's friend, and pride and joy. In the summer she lived in a hutch in his shed on the allotments, and he would spend his days sitting with her.

Dale cradled the limp body of Bonnie in his arms and walked back to Mr. Hamilton. "I'm so sorry, sir. I wish we could've saved her."

Fresh tears spilled over as Mr. Hamilton awkwardly held out his hands for the rabbit. "You tried, son. You did your best." Dale glanced at the paramedic, who shrugged, and Dale placed her in Mr. Hamilton's lap. Mr. Hamilton gently stroked Bonnie's fur. "You were the best, old girl."

Dale had to blink back tears of his own, touched by the old man's grief. "Is there anything I can do for you?"

Mr. Hamilton shook his head. "We're fine, son. Thanks for asking."

Tank waved at Dale, attracting his attention, and pointed down the path. Ben strode toward them. Dale hadn't expected to see him, but then nothing much happened in the village that Ben didn't know about.

"What happened here?" Ben asked as he joined them.

"We're all fine, except for poor Bonnie." Dale nodded at the limp rabbit on Mr. Hamilton's lap.

"My Bonnie didn't make it." Mr. Hamilton petted Bonnie's fur.

Ben knelt by his chair. "I am so sorry, Mr. Hamilton."

"She was my family, Mr. Ben." Another tear traced a sooty path down Mr. Hamilton's cheek.

"I know she was, sir," Ben murmured, and Dale noticed how gentle he was with the old man. "Are you hurt?"

"Burns and scrapes to his hands," Dale said. "He couldn't open the door to get to her."

"I have to talk to the fire officers, Mr. Hamilton, but I'll be back in a moment. Colson's going to be here with a cup of tea for you."

Ben stood and they moved away from the grieving man. Ben growled under his breath. "I'll take Mrs. Wilson to visit him this afternoon. She's one of his friends."

Dale managed a yawn as a response. "I'm sorry. Christ, I'm tired."

Ben made a worried sound. "You sound exhausted. I'll pick you up after your shift."

"I'm not really feeling that sociable, babe. I'm off tomorrow. I could come around then."

"You need food and sleep tonight," Ben said. "Let me take care of you."

"You don't have to—"

"Shut up," Ben snapped.

Dale smiled wearily at his bossiness. "Okay, I'll see you later."

"Maloney, hurry up," Tank yelled.

Ben brushed his hand, and then Dale left. The last sight he had as they drove away was Mr. Hamilton sitting in a folding chair, Bonnie still in his lap, and Ben sitting next to him, a comforting hand on Mr. Hamilton's arm.

DALE flopped wearily onto the sofa in the fire station break room, glad to close his eyes for five minutes. "Christ, I'm knackered."

Tank grunted something incoherent from one of the chairs. Mick was facedown on the other sofa and didn't bother to say anything. The others had disappeared, and no one felt like talking.

"Maloney, a word please."

Dale opened his eyes to see the station commander in the doorway. "Yes, sir." He tried to hide a yawn as he walked into Fang's office. "Is everything okay?"

"Sit down, Maloney."

Dale sat in front of the desk, searching his brain for what he'd done wrong.

Fang took his time before he spoke. "How long have you been here now?"

Dale thought for a moment. "Uh, four weeks?"

"And have you settled in? I know you got some hazing at the beginning."

"Nothing I can't handle."

"Good, good." Fang took a long time before he spoke again. "Lord Calminster…."

"Yes?" Dale said warily.

"You and he seem to be friends."

"Yes."

"I've been here five years, and you're the first person I've seen him relax with," Fang said.

Dale forced a smile. "He's a nice guy."

Fang's lips twitched. "I'm sure he is."

"What is it you're worried about?" Dale wanted Fang to come to the point.

"What makes you think I'm worried?"

Dale held back his eye roll with an effort. "I'm in your office with the door closed. Something is bothering you. You don't like that I'm friends with Ben?"

"Are you friends or… something else?"

Dale stared coldly at his station commander. "With all due respect, sir, that's none of your business."

"With all due respect, Maloney," Fang snapped, "anything that affects this station is my fucking business.

You're here five minutes, and now you've got your feet under the table of the lord of the manor."

"Are you worried about me or this station?"

Fang exhaled a sharp breath. "I don't mind who you make friends with, but did it have to be Lord Calminster?"

"He's a really nice guy, and he's lonely." Dale huffed. "Who the hell else has made friends with him in the village?"

"He mixes in different social circles to the rest of us."

"Maybe it's about time that changed."

Fang shook his head. "No matter how *nice* he is, Calminster isn't one of us. If he gets pissed off, he could do us a great deal of harm."

Dale pressed his lips together, holding back the angry words before he talked himself out of a job. "Is that all?"

"That's all." As Dale stalked to the door, Fang spoke again. "Dale, just be careful, okay? And if you need to talk, my door is always open."

Dale didn't trust himself to respond.

Tank glanced up as Dale entered the kitchen. "You okay, Maloney?"

"No!" Dale said shortly.

"You want to talk about it?"

"No," Dale headed for the kettle, "but thanks for asking."

Tank nodded. "Make us a cuppa."

Before they'd even finished their tea, they were called back out for another fire, this time in a shed full of wheelie bins at the back of the local school.

"We've got to catch this idiot," Tank growled as they drove back to the station.

"He's escalating," Mick said. "We're just lucky no one's been badly hurt."

"Have you noticed all of the latest fires only started after Mrs. Wilson's fire?" Dale said.

"You think it's connected?" Tank asked.

"The cottage fire was an accident," Dale said. "But these others have been dumpsters and garden sheds. Small stuff. I wonder if the arsonist saw the cottage fire and decided to try his hand. Start small, work his way up to something big."

"I'll talk to Dan Verne. See if he's heard anything," Tank said.

Dale knew Verne was the police constable who covered Calminster village, but he hadn't met him so far.

Mick snorted. "You'd get more information in the Crook." Mick didn't have a very high opinion of the local copper.

"Someone's going to get badly hurt soon," Dale said.

"Someone did," Tank pointed out. "Poor Bonnie. She was Mr. Hamilton's best friend."

"The fires only started when you moved into the village, Dale." Mick's grin confirmed he wasn't being serious.

Still, Dale growled because he was the last person to start stupid fires. "It ain't me."

"We know that, snowflake." Tank cuffed him lightly around the head.

"Watch it!" Dale ducked, nearly crashing into equipment.

"Kids, break it up!" It was Mick's turn to growl as the bickering distracted him.

They settled down, but still, it played on Dale's mind enough that he forgot Ben was picking him up. Dale was halfway down the main road leading into the village when he jumped out of his skin as a car horn sounded next to him. He looked around, a scowl on his face, only to fade as he saw Ben waving at him. The Land Rover stopped and Dale got in.

"Did you forget I was picking you up?" Ben said as he pulled away, an apologetic wave at the car behind for holding them up.

"You were?"

"We spoke? Earlier, at the allotments?"

Dale groaned as he remembered. "I'm sorry. There was another fire, and it went right out of my head."

Ben frowned. "Another one?"

"Yeah, at the school. No casualties this time. Hey, we've just passed my road."

"I know. You're coming back to mine. Shut up and don't argue," Ben said as Dale opened his mouth.

Much as Dale liked the Hall, all he really wanted was the quiet of his cottage and his own bed. Still, Ben meant well, and it would be nice to spend some time with him. Dale yawned and closed his eyes for a moment. The next thing Dale knew, Ben was shaking him awake.

"Hey, Dale, wakey-wakey."

Annoyed at being disturbed, Dale moaned and tried to thump his pillow.

"Come on, grumpy. You can't sleep here."

Dale blinked and sat up. "Wha…? Did I fall asleep?"

Ben rolled his eyes. "You'd better have been asleep. Otherwise you snore when you're awake."

"I don't snore."

"Of course you don't, Dale." Ben said it in the most condescending tone he could manage.

Dale grumbled under his breath and reluctantly got out of the Land Rover. He was so tired, he was tempted to ask Ben to leave him there for a couple of hours.

Ben must have realized how tired Dale was feeling because he came around the vehicle and slung his arm around Dale's waist. "Come on, let's get you into bed."

"I thought you were going to feed me."

"I am, but you can eat in bed."

He guided Dale into the Hall, shushing away the dogs when they swarmed around them, begging for attention. Tiredly, Dale bent down and patted each dog; then he let Ben take him upstairs.

In Ben's bedroom, Ben pushed Dale to sit down on the bed. Dale went to take his T-shirt off, but Ben stayed him. "Let me. You just sit."

Dale let Ben take off his shoes and undress him. Maybe it should have felt odd being undressed like a child, but Dale was too tired to care. Once Dale was naked, Ben encouraged him to stand briefly and pulled back the covers. Dale snuggled onto the pillows, and Ben covered him.

"I'll bring you food shortly," Ben said.

Dale mumbled that he'd better and was out like a light.

THE light had changed in the bedroom when Dale surfaced again. He opened his eyes, blinking in the soft glow from the bedside lamp.

"Hey. You're awake." Ben took his headphones off and smiled at him.

"What time is it?" Dale squinted at the clock.

"Just gone ten."

"I guess I missed dinner."

Ben chuckled. "Did you really think you were going to stay awake long enough to eat?"

"Guess not." Dale sat up and yawned, scratching his armpit.

"Are you hungry?"

"A bit." Dale's stomach growled. "Starving."

Ben hopped out of bed and brought over a tray. "Lisa made you a sandwich."

Dale tried to hide his disappointment because he was hungry; then Ben took the lid off the plate, and Dale's stomach rumbled in appreciation. "That's not a sandwich. It's a skyscraper."

"She didn't want you to be hungry."

Dale didn't bother to reply. He had a mouthful of freshly baked bread and roast beef.

Ben let Dale hoover his way through two sandwiches and salad and crisps, plus some of Mrs. Wilson's carrot cake, before he spoke. "Feeling better?"

Dale belched loudly.

"I take it that's a yes."

"I'm stuffed." Dale burped again.

"Classy! Do you want a drink?"

"I could murder a cup of tea."

Ben leaned over and switched the kettle on. Dale had been amused the first time he realized Ben had a kettle and a fridge in his room, but he'd quickly grown to appreciate that traversing two flights of stairs to the kitchen in the Hall was not the same as walking the short distance in his cottage. In a couple of minutes, he slurped happily at a cup of hot tea.

Ben leaned back against the pillows and encouraged Dale to rest against him while they drank their tea. "It's good to have you here. I miss you when you go home."

Dale tended to stay overnight at the cottage while he was on his four days "on," and then he'd spend most of his time at the Hall on his days off. "I miss you too." His cottage was fine for his needs, but he'd not spent enough time in it to feel like home.

"You could stay here all the time."

Dale tilted his head to gaze at Ben. "You're asking me to move in with you?"

"Is it a bit soon?"

"Maybe. I'd have to think about it."

Silence fell between them, but it didn't feel odd to Dale. Ben had laid his cards on the table. Now it was up to Dale to think about it. He didn't want to rush into anything, especially after Baz, but he wouldn't dismiss the idea altogether.

Ben took Dale's cup out of his hand when he'd finished and manhandled him until he could wrap himself around Dale. Dale wasn't keen on being the little spoon. Still, it was nice to be taken care of once in a while.

"Are you tired?" Ben asked.

"Not too much now."

"Do you want to tell me what's bothering you?" Ben caressed Dale's hair.

Dale yawned again. "What makes you think something's bothering me?"

Ben held Dale a little tighter. "You said something in the car."

"I was asleep. What did I say?"

"You said 'It wasn't me. I didn't do it.'"

"I've no idea."

"Sure?" Ben seemed determined to get an answer.

Dale thought about it for a moment. "I guess it might have been a throwaway remark by Tank."

"What did he say?"

"That the fires didn't start until I joined the station."

"What the hell?" Ben's fingers tightened in Dale's hair.

"He was joking."

"He'd better be." Ben sounded fierce, which made Dale smile, pleased at Ben's passionate defense.

"You going to ride in like a white knight? Defend my honor?"

"If I have to." Dale laughed and pushed back against Ben, who held him tighter. After a few minutes, when Dale was on the edge of sleep again, Ben whispered, "What if it's one of us?"

That snapped Dale back to consciousness. "Starting the fires?"

"Yes. It's got to be someone local."

Dale rolled over onto his back, noticing the worried expression on Ben's face. "The small fires are the sort of the thing teenagers get up to. They're bored, think it's a laugh to get the fire service involved. We have to come out no matter how big the fire."

"But it's constant since Mrs. Wilson's fire?" Ben asked.

"It feels like it. I guess the village is usually quiet."

"We had a spate of vandalism before, and once we had a murder."

Dale stared at Ben. "No way! A murder?"

Ben gave him a wry smile. "Mark Jones. He was stabbed three years ago."

"What the hell? Did you catch the guy?"

"Woman," Ben corrected.

"He was murdered by a woman?"

"Tessa was his girlfriend. He'd promised her he would leave his wife, but he was stringing her along.

He was drinking in the Shepherd's Crook when she came in and stabbed him in the neck."

"Fuck. Poor bloke."

Ben shrugged. "I don't have much sympathy for him."

"That's not like you."

"I was at school with him. He was a dick then."

"Did he bully you?"

"Sometimes. Most of the time he left me alone. His wife was devastated, first by the murder, and then finding out he'd been cheating on her."

"Christ, it really is *Midsomer Murders*."

"It's just one murder in the last fifty years. I don't think the police have a lot of excitement. I'm sure you saw more in your last job."

"Some," Dale admitted. "I'd be happy never to see another dead body."

Some of the things Dale had seen haunted his dreams. He'd never needed to explain his nightmares to Baz because he'd seen the same horrors. Dale wasn't ready to share his nightmares with Ben just yet.

Ben bent down and kissed him. "You're a hero."

"Bollocks! It's my job." Dale had been told this many times, but he never saw it like that. He was just doing his job.

"You're a hero. My hero." Ben kissed him again to emphasize his point.

Dale groaned into Ben's mouth, enfolding Ben in his embrace. Ben could call him the Cookie Monster for all Dale cared. They kissed for a long time, but Dale had to admit in the end he was too tired to take things further.

"That's okay," Ben said as he switched off the bedside light and settled down with his head on Dale's chest. "There's always tomorrow."

Dale was almost asleep when he felt Ben stroke his belly. "I'm not a dog, you know."

"Huh?"

"You're stroking my stomach."

Ben chuckled, his breath warm against Dale's skin. "I've got a thing for hairy bellies."

"You're just weird," Dale murmured.

"I know." Ben pressed a kiss into Dale's chest and settled down again.

Dale smiled, unseen in the darkness. Weird was just fine with him.

Chapter Twelve

BEN sat at the long table at the front of the church hall, conscious of all eyes upon him. This wasn't the first village meeting he'd held, and it wouldn't be the last. He was joined by PC Dan Verne and the fire station commander, Lee Fang. The vicar of the local parish church sat on the end of the table. Ben had as little to do with Rosemary Taylor as he could manage, having discovered the woman's homophobic tendencies. The previous vicar had been the most inclusive man Ben had ever known. The same, unfortunately, couldn't be said for his replacement. Ben knew she was unaware why he avoided her. Maybe soon the reason would be in Rosemary's face.

He watched as the hall slowly filled with the villagers, people shaking off the persistent evening rain as they came in the door. An array of damp umbrellas sat by the doors, waiting to be collected on the way out. Dale was already there, sitting at the back with Tank and Mick. The usual suspects took up the front rows, and the rest of the villagers filed in behind. Ben nodded at Mrs. Wilson and Mr. Hamilton, who walked in together with Mr. Colson. Ben would have liked Dale to sit by his side. He snorted to himself at the thought of Dale being introduced as his spouse to the village. Ben could imagine Dale running in horror, and he snorted again. Lee Fang glanced at him curiously.

"Hay fever," Ben said, using the first excuse he could think of.

Fang nodded. "Ah. Allergies are a pain in the arse."

Ben decided not to explain that he'd actually been thinking of someone he'd rather have in his arse.

When the hall was full, Rosemary stood and called everyone to attention. She had a penetrating voice that cut through the chatter, and soon the noise subsided. She looked over at Ben.

"Lord Calminster, do you want to start?"

Ben got to his feet. "Thank you, Reverend Taylor. Good evening, everyone. Thank you for coming out this evening. I know the weather is horrible. I hope this won't take long." He paused and looked to where Dale sat, his arms folded. Just Dale's presence gave him strength. "We all know the number of fires in the village is escalating. I'm grateful we have a manned fire station on our doorstep." Ben looked at Mr. Hamilton. "I'm so sorry about Bonnie, Mr. Hamilton." There was a murmur of agreement among the crowd, and Mrs. Wilson patted the old man's knee. Ben looked sternly at the crowd. "If this is the work of one person, it needs to stop right now, before someone gets hurt." He didn't believe for one moment that the arsonist was in the hall, but he hoped to appeal to anyone who might have information that could lead to their capture. The crowd stared back at him, and he sighed inwardly. "I'll let PC Verne and Station Commander Fang take over with practical advice. In the meantime, my door is always open to anyone who wants to talk to me confidentially."

Ben sat down and looked over at Dale, who sent him a smile. He spent the next hour making an effort to pay attention and not to stare at Dale the whole time, although he had a feeling he failed when he caught Colson rolling his eyes at him.

At the end of the meeting, he made his escape as quickly as he could, knowing people would relax once he left. Shivering in the cold night air, Ben walked out of the church grounds onto the green. He wasn't sure what had happened to Dale until a shadow emerged from the darkness of the trees.

"I wondered where you'd got to," Ben said as he walked toward Dale.

"I thought I'd go before anyone noticed." Dale held out his hand to tug him closer. "You're shivering."

"It's cold and raining, or haven't you noticed?" Ben shuddered as raindrops ran down the back of his neck.

Dale brushed Ben's lips. "I don't notice anything when you're around."

Although the hall was full of people, Ben knew he and Dale were sufficiently sheltered, and he reached up for a kiss. Dale was passive for a moment, as if he was surprised; then he gave a low growl in his throat and hauled Ben against him. The sudden action made Ben stumble, and arms flailing, he fell into Dale, who landed on his back with Ben plastered atop him. Momentarily stunned, Ben lay on top of Dale, who hadn't made a sound beside a grunt.

"There must be dryer places to do that."

To Ben's horror, those were the dry tones of Station Commander Fang. He looked up to discover Fang and Verne staring down at them.

"Oh fucking hell," Dale gasped in his ear.

"I—I…." Ben scrambled off Dale and got to his feet.

Dale stayed where he was for a moment, and Ben started to worry he'd seriously hurt Dale when he grunted again. "Help me up?" Ben and Fang pulled Dale to his feet. He rubbed the small of his back. "I didn't expect that to happen. You're bloody heavy."

"What did—no, I don't want to know," Verne muttered.

"What did you want?" Ben asked, grateful for the darkness covering his wildly flaming cheeks.

"Could we have a quick word, your lordship?" Fang said.

Dale had told Ben about his chat with the station commander about their "friendship." Ben could only imagine how Dale must be feeling at this moment. He glanced at Dale, who stared at the ground, like he was praying for it to open up and swallow him.

"I'm going home for a hot shower and dry clothes. Give me a call later?" Dale raised an eyebrow at Ben.

"Yes, I will." Ben watched Dale limp off toward his cottage and then realized Verne and Fang were still waiting for his attention. He took a steadying breath and smiled tightly at the men. "I'm sorry about that. What do you want to talk about?"

His brows knitted together, Fang stared after his retreating officer before he spoke again. "We just wanted to talk about the meeting."

A WEEK later, Ben shivered as he crossed Charing Cross Road toward the station. For nearly the end of April, it was bloody cold, and he'd forgotten his thick jacket. He'd had two days of meetings with the shareholders of Calminster Enterprises, trying to put out the fires Barrett kept trying to start. Dale had promised to come with him; then at the last moment he got asked to cover shifts for a fire officer whose mother had died. Ben could hardly make a fuss, but he desperately missed Dale's presence. They'd known each other for mere weeks, yet Ben felt like they'd known each other forever. At some point they were going to have to consummate the relationship. Between the arsonist and Ben's business problems, the lack of time was putting a serious kink in their sex life.

He went through the ticket barrier, dodging a couple with huge wheeled suitcases and a group of students oblivious to anyone else but themselves. The tube station was crowded, as usual, but at least he was out of the wind. He was on his way to have lunch with Edmund Freely, his other major shareholder apart from Barrett, and an old friend of his father. Freely had been supportive since Ben's father died, but that was when he thought Ben was going to marry Sabrina. Freely was old-school Catholic, and Barrett hadn't hesitated in telling everyone why Ben had parted company with Sabrina. Most of the shareholders couldn't care less where he dipped his wick—if only he was that lucky—as one of them phrased it, but Freely was another matter. He'd invited Ben to lunch—less an invite and more a summons—and made it plain it would be unwise to refuse.

Another blast of cold wind left Ben shivering as he walked down the road to the Freely & Sons office. He was about to step into the building when his phone vibrated in his pocket.

"Morning, babe." Dale's low growl made Ben shiver again but for an entirely different reason. "I've got a break, so I thought I'd call you."

"Good timing," Ben said. "I've just reached Freely's."

"How did the other meetings go?"

"All fine. One or two thought I was mad for dumping Sabrina, but when I said she was my lawyer now, they thought it was a much better relationship."

"Your ex has got a reputation."

"You have no idea."

"When am I going to meet her?"

Ben rubbed his eyes. "Soon." *Never.*

Dale chuckled. "You really don't want me to meet Sabrina, do you?"

"You worked that out?"

"It's going to happen eventually, Ben."

"Eventually is a long while, my friend, and the longer the better." The thought of Dale and Sabrina in the same room made Ben shudder every time he thought about it.

"Wuss!"

"I have no idea what you mean," Ben said haughtily.

"You went all Lord Calminster there."

"Huh!"

"It turns me on. Like when you laid into me about the pole." Dale's voice dropped an octave.

"It did?" Ben asked skeptically.

"Oh yeah. I still get a boner thinking about it."

The last thing Ben needed was getting hard just at the thought of Dale getting a boner. "I'm going."

"Is there a problem?" Dale snickered in his ear.

"I am not facing my deeply religious business partner with a hard-on." A woman who had just left the building gave Ben a shocked glance. "And a woman overheard me talking about hard-ons."

Dale burst out laughing.

"I'm glad you find it amusing," Ben snapped.

"Oh come on, it is funny."

Ben wasn't in the mood to be coaxed. "No, it's not."

"It is. Just a little bit."

"Maybe a bit," Ben admitted. Then he caught sight of a clock in the reception. "I've got to go, Dale. I'll call you when I'm out."

"It'll be fine. Just summon your inner lordship."

"However did I manage before I met you?" Ben said, snark in his tone.

"I have no idea."

"Go away!"

"You're the one that has to go."

Ben disconnected the call. "Heh! Watch me go." Sometimes summoning a teenage girl was just as good.

The blast of hot air as Ben entered the building was welcome. He strode over to the reception.

A young man at the desk welcomed him to the building. "Good morning, sir. May I help you?"

"Ben Raleigh to see Mr. Freely," Ben said.

"Lord Calminster, Mr. Freely is expecting you. Jessica will be down in a moment. Why don't you take a seat over there?" The man indicated the sofas in one corner of the large lobby area.

Ben wasn't surprised the man knew his title. He knew Freely well enough to be aware reception would have been briefed about his arrival. Freely owned the whole building, and the only companies that used the floors were his in some way. Ben admired Freely, if not some of his practices for running his company. He hoped to be as successful, although he would never work in London. Ben was just as happy working from the countryside and making brief trips into the city.

He sat on the sofa as people scurried past the building. It had started to rain, and they kept their heads down against the inclement weather.

"Lord Calminster?"

Ben looked up to see Freely's PA smiling at him. He'd known Jessica most of his life, as she'd been with Freely for over thirty years. Personally, Ben had no idea how she could work for the man, but she was devoted to him, probably even more so than his wife, who spent most of her time abroad.

"Jessica, it's good to see you again." Ben stood and shook her hand.

"Mr. Freely is still in his last meeting, but he asked me to take you to the conference room."

Jessica led him to the lifts. No visitor was allowed to roam the building without a member of staff with them. The lift took them swiftly to the fifteenth floor, which housed the executive conference rooms.

"Would you like a coffee?"

"Yes, please." Ben sat down in the leather armchair. "Do you know how long Mr. Freely will be?"

"I'm afraid I don't. If you'd like to work, the room has Wi-Fi."

"Great. I'll do that."

"I'll bring you your coffee." She smiled and vanished out of the room.

Ben sighed. He didn't want to spend all day at Freely's. He'd hoped to have lunch and return back to the Hall for a dinner with Dale. But he couldn't skip out on the meeting either. He pulled out his iPad and brought up his schedule. He needed to prepare for a new programme they were starting next year for teenagers in the village. He wanted something similar to what he had in place for the ex-prisoners, where they received training rather than being handed a duster or a hoe and told to get on with it. His staff were on board with the idea, but the problem was deciding what training they should receive.

Then he needed to take time with one of his smaller companies that wasn't doing so well. It made garden equipment by hand for the specialized user. They were luxury goods, and he knew he was feeding a dying market. But some of the people had been working there since his father's time. To shut it down would have consequences for a lot of them. Ben sighed. He loved running the businesses, but he hated making tough decisions that involved making people redundant. That was the difference between him and Barrett or Freely. Neither of them had any hesitation in winding up a business that wasn't making a profit. To them it was just that, business.

Jessica came in with the coffeepot. "Mr. Freely says he'll be about fifteen minutes. I've arranged lunch for 12:30 in the Blue room."

"Thank you," Ben murmured.

She smiled and left him alone to go to her desk. He knew if he needed anything, he only had to call.

He sat down and reviewed the nonprofit programmes for teenagers. Before Freely came into the room, Ben had a good idea which skills he thought they should be training the kids in. All of them were something that they could take into the outside world. Ben was a firm believer that not every child was academic. Although he'd enjoyed studying, his sister had hated school and couldn't wait to leave. She now ran her own company, very successfully. In fact, Ben often asked for her advice because she had a sound business mind.

The door opened and Freely strode in. "Benedict, my boy, good to see you."

Ben stood and held out his hand. "Uncle Edmund, how are you?"

"Oh, doing well. Jessica?" Freely yelled for his PA.

She hurried into the room. "Yes, Mr. Freely?"

"More coffee for us both, please, and biscuits. I'm starving."

Ben cleared away his work, and they sat. He waited for Freely to speak, knowing the man was giving him a speculative look.

"Barrett came to see me."

"I thought he would," Ben said calmly.

"He's not happy with you."

"I know that too."

Freely huffed and stopped talking as Jessica came back in with a tray. She poured the coffee and left the biscuits, quietly leaving the room. Ben was relieved. If this was a serious meeting, she would have stayed. The fact that she left meant Freely had something to say, but it wasn't essential.

"He told me about you and Sabrina."

Ben said nothing.

"Glad to see you came to your senses."

Ben stared at him. That was the last thing he'd expected Freely to say. "You don't mind?"

"Sabrina would have eaten you alive."

"You know she's my lawyer now?"

Freely gave a smirk. "I'd heard. Barrett is spitting feathers."

"She's a good lawyer."

"She is. That's why Freely & Sons have her on retainer."

Ben snorted into his coffee cup. No wonder she'd been so sure of Freely's reaction. "She didn't tell me that."

"I don't pay her to have a loose tongue. Bradshaw, Logan, and Winslet has been working for us since she set up the new firm."

"Why did you hire her? I thought you and Barrett had issues?" Ben asked.

Freely smiled. "She told you that, did she?"

Ben shrugged. "Was it a secret?"

"No. I told her to tell you. Barrett is an oik who's done well for himself. I'm not a snob…."

Ben grinned inwardly because he'd never met a bigger snob than Freely. "You don't like him."

"I don't like the way he works, and I don't like the way he treats people."

"You have to admit he's good at business. He started Barrett and Barrett with nothing. Barrett Media and Leisure is one of the top in the industry." Ben couldn't help the dig, as Freely had inherited his business as Ben had. Both had done well, but Ben always acknowledged he had a head start in life.

The dig obviously went over Freely's head, or he ignored it, because he just carried on. "Barrett wants me to sell my shares to him."

Ben frowned. "Why would he need to do that?"

"He's determined to have you by the balls, Ben. You not only rejected his daughter. You rejected all the plans he had."

"I told him I was happy for two of our businesses to merge."

"He still wants Calminster Enterprises, the estate, and the Hall," Freely said.

"I told him that wasn't going to happen."

Freely shrugged. "You may have said that, but it's not what he heard."

"There is no way he's getting his hands on my home to make his"—Ben pulled a face—"art-nouveau-designed hotel or whatever crap he has in mind." Maybe Ben did have a touch of snobbery about him, but Calminster Hall was his ancestral home, not a fucking hotel for Barrett's golf buddies.

"You know I agree with you."

"So you told him you weren't going to sell?"

"Not exactly."

Ben stared at him. "What exactly?"

"Sabrina suggested I play the long game with Barrett. Let him think I'm interested."

"Keep your friends close and your enemies closer?" Ben murmured.

Freely inclined his head. "I've always found it a wise strategy."

"And what about the fact I'm gay?"

Freely's mouth tightened. "I assume nothing I can say will make a difference to your actions."

"I'm not going back into the closet again," Ben said.

"Then I see little point talking about it."

"But you don't approve."

"My approval is irrelevant, Benedict. I cannot agree with your lifestyle choice. However, you are the son of my closest friend, and a good businessman. I don't want to force you out of my life. Let's leave it there."

And, like that, Ben knew the matter was closed. There was no point pushing the discussion anymore. Freely didn't approve, but he would ignore it for the sake of their relationship, and Ben had to take it or leave it. He chose to accept it—for business and because Freely was almost family.

"Shall we have lunch?" Freely asked. "Then we can discuss what to do with Barrett."

Ben got to his feet. "Do you have any ideas?"

"I always have ideas, my boy. However, most of them aren't legal."

"No wonder you retained Sabrina. You're two of a kind."

"Let's eat." Freely guided Ben out of the room. "You'll feel better after panfried trout. I caught them myself."

"I'm honored."

"Of course you are. I'd expect nothing less."

Chapter Thirteen

DALE squinted at his phone again. Ben's text was cryptic, to say the least.

2pm. Left at the end of the Long Walk, walk towards the Rose Garden, round the old lord, and look right.

Ben had left Dale to sleep in while he disappeared downstairs to work, but while Dale was asleep, Ben had sent him a text.

"What the hell is the old lord?" Dale muttered as he surveyed the Rose Garden.

"Over there. The bust of the first Lord Calminster."

Dale jumped as Tim spoke. He hadn't noticed Tim approach him from behind. "Jesus, don't do that!"

"Sorry. You sounded lost." Tim grinned at him. Okay, the grin was more of a smirk, but Dale ignored him.

"Ben—Lord Calminster—sent me a text."

"He's up there." Tim pointed to a round stone blob that looked nothing like a human. *Right at the old lord.*

"Cheers."

Dale loped up the path, but there was still no sign of Ben. He reached the weatherworn stone bench. "Ben?" he said, a touch uncertain now.

"Hi." Ben emerged between two yew hedges. "Finally."

"Hey." Dale took a long look at Ben, who was wearing an open-necked blue shirt and jeans, one or two hairs showing above the vee of the shirt. He smiled at Ben and held out his arms. Ben stepped into them and they kissed. Dale licked his lips. "You taste of wine."

"I've been waiting awhile," Ben admitted. "I opened the bottle."

"Sorry, I was lost."

"Did Tim find you?"

"You put him there?"

Ben grinned. "Just in case."

Dale huffed, but he wasn't that mad. "I thought you were feeding me."

"I am." Ben took Dale's hand and drew him through the gap in the hedges. "And if you're lucky—"

"Fuck me!" Dale stared at the scene before him. Rugs and cushions were laid out, with a wicker basket to one side, and two glasses of wine, one of them half-full.

"Later." Ben smirked. "Let's eat first."

He tugged Dale down, and they made themselves comfortable on the cushions. Ben opened the wicker basket, and Dale's jaw dropped.

"My idea of a picnic is a sandwich and a packet of crisps from Sainsbury's, maybe Marks and Spencer if I'm splashing out."

Ben snorted. "Mrs. Wilson would kill me if I bought a sandwich." He unloaded the chicken, beef, freshly made bread, salad, homemade coleslaw, pies—

"How many people are coming to the picnic?" Dale asked.

"Just you and me. She wasn't sure what you'd eat, so she packed everything."

Dale shook his head. "Mrs. Wilson is amazing."

"She is. I'm glad she's back."

Mrs. Wilson had insisted she start work again, although Lisa was there, by her side, if she needed help. Ben had confided to Dale that he didn't know how long Mrs. Wilson would be able to cope, but no one was going to deny her the chance to work as long as she wanted.

Ben handed Dale a plate. "Fill it up."

Dale loaded his plate with meat and salad, and Ben gave him a hunk of bread. They didn't talk for a while, beyond the odd moans as Dale took the first mouthful of Mrs. Wilson's cooking. Eventually Dale declared he couldn't eat another morsel.

"That's a shame," Ben said.

"Why?"

Ben reached into the basket and pulled out a container full of strawberries and grapes, and a smaller pot of dark chocolate sauce. "I thought we could feed each other and then get on with the fucking. Colson is under orders not to disturb us."

Dale was never one to ignore a challenge. "Give me five minutes and then you're on."

They piled away the rest of the food back into the basket, banked the cushions, and lay back for a while to let the huge lunch settle.

Ben snuggled against Dale. "I miss you when you work nights."

"I miss you too." Dale inhaled the fresh citrus scent of Ben's hair and held him closer. "Mick's just not as much fun as you."

"Arse."

"Don't hit me or I'll hurl," Dale warned.

"I haven't got the energy to hit you. Maybe later."

Dale stroked Ben's hair. "You sound tired."

"I was working most of the night. Barrett's causing trouble again."

"I thought Sabrina was dealing with him."

Ben sighed. "She is."

"I'm sorry, Ben. Why is he being such an arsehole?"

"He's not used to anyone saying no." Ben rolled onto his side and looked at Dale. "I damaged his business and his ego. He thought he had me tied up in a neat little bundle. I'd marry Sabrina. He'd get his hands on my business, the Hall, and my position in society. When I broke off the relationship, I was saying no to him, not Sabrina. I've met a lot of men like him. Money brings power but it doesn't always bring status, and that's what he wants."

Dale worried his bottom lip for a moment before he spoke. "You know I don't give a shit about that, don't you?"

"What?" Ben asked.

"Status. Money and status."

"You're worried I think you're a gold-digger?"

Dale nodded. "I've got nothing except my house back in Nottingham and some savings."

Ben sat up, sitting cross-legged to face Dale. "And I've got status, money, and a title?"

"What can I offer you—apart from the obvious?" Dale added at Ben's wicked expression.

"My staff like you."

"That's nice," Dale said, not sure why that was relevant.

Ben traced a random path over Dale's thighs, which was distracting to say the least. "They've never liked anyone before, and I mean *anyone*. You, they liked from the start. Yeah, it occurred to all of us you might be interested in me for the money."

"So what makes me different?" Dale really wanted to know what Ben saw in him.

Ben counted them off on his fingers. "You have integrity and morals. You didn't like Baz cheating. You didn't like the thought I was using Sabrina. You immediately offered to repair the maypole. You were prepared to throw Barrett out for me. You hated even the idea that you were responsible for the fires—"

Dale chuckled. "Okay, I get the gist. You like me."

"More than *like* you, sweetheart." Ben's gaze grew heated.

He reached over, picked a strawberry from the container, and dipped it in the sauce, then used it to trace Dale's lips. Dale's cock thickened in his jeans as Ben leaned forward to lick away the sweetness. Ben repeated the action, and Dale licked his lips this time; then Ben fed him the strawberry. Dale bit into it, closing his mouth around Ben's fingertips. Their gazes locked on each other.

Dale rested his hands on Ben's hips. Neither of them moved for a long while. Then Ben kissed him again. Dale made a noise deep in his throat, and still kissing him, he wrapped his arms around Ben, rolling him over until Ben was on his back. He wanted Ben and he wanted him now. He straddled Ben's hips and leaned forward to undo the top button of Ben's shirt. Ben grabbed his hands, and Dale paused.

"Do you want me to stop?" It suddenly occurred to Dale that Ben might not want to fuck there, where anyone could interrupt them.

"I wanted to check you were okay."

Dale was touched. "I'm fine, and I really need to fuck."

Ben gave a shaky laugh. "Oh God, me too."

He let go of Dale's hands, and Dale undid the buttons, pushing the shirt aside to look at him. A crimson flush spread up Ben's chest and throat. He was stunning; all lean muscle and a light smattering of dark hair. Dale devoured his fill and then helped Ben take off the rest of his clothes.

"Are you going to get undressed?" Ben asked when Dale made no move to strip.

"Not yet." Dale wanted to savor the moment.

Dale felt the tension thrumming through Ben's muscles, but he was aroused, his long dick hard and glistening at the tip.

"I want to see you." Ben almost whined in anticipation.

Dale stood and stripped off his clothes. Maybe he gave Ben more of a show than usual, but he didn't take his time.

"You're—" Ben stared at Dale's cock with a hungry expression on his face. "Hurry up."

Dale jacked his dick a couple of times, pulling the foreskin back for Ben to get a proper look. He smeared the drop of precome resting in the slit over the head. Ben got to his knees and leaned forward, his mouth at Dale's cock. He didn't take; he asked so nicely. Dale smeared Ben's lips with his precome, and Dale nearly shot his load at the pretty sight of Ben's glistening mouth.

"Jesus!" Dale bent down and licked the taste of himself from Ben's lips.

Ben stayed passive for a moment; then he sat back on his heels. "I want your cock in my mouth."

Dale raised an eyebrow. "Are you asking or demanding?"

In response, Ben got back on his hands and knees and opened his mouth, and Dale's dick decided it didn't care what the answer was. It just wanted to sink into that warm cavern and play the hokey-cokey. Dale tangled his fingers in Ben's hair and guided them both until Ben's mouth was around the head. Ben's blue eyes were huge and his lips stretched thin around the shaft.

"You look fucking amazing," Dale whispered and gently touched Ben's cheek, feeling himself in there. Ben hummed, and the vibrations went through Dale. He had to close his eyes and recite the seven-times table just to hold on to what little control he had.

Ben pulled back and licked over the glans, making sure he caught the sensitive part just under the head. Dale sank into the sensation of Ben's magical touch until it wasn't enough. He needed more.

"Suck it," Dale ordered.

Once again, Ben sank around Dale's dick until Dale could feel the throat muscles tickling the sensitive tip. Dale stared questioningly down at Ben, who nodded. He grabbed Ben's head and started to fuck his mouth, not slamming into the back of Ben's throat but needing to control the rhythm. It was messy and fabulous, and Dale didn't take long before he felt his balls tighten and his body prepare to climax. He'd expected to fuck Ben, but he couldn't wait. He came with a shout, his back arching, and pumping into Ben's mouth with abandon. Ben took it all, took him and the come spurting out of Dale's dick like he was made for Dale.

Dale had heard the phrase "his brain shot out of his dick" but he'd never actually experienced it until this moment. Ben had taken everything he had to offer and then some. When Ben finally let him go, Dale slumped forward. Ben guided him back to the cushions and snuggled next to him.

"Your turn," Dale mumbled, feeling a hot, swollen shaft against his belly. "Gonna have to wait a minute. Body off-line."

Ben chuckled. "Don't take too long. I've got plans for you." His voice sounded hoarse and well used.

Dale cracked open one eye. "What plans?"

"Wait and see."

The smug tone would have worried Dale if he could've worked up the energy. Finally, he felt the strength returning to his limbs and his dick, just about the time Ben started humping his belly, slivers of precome painting Dale's skin. "Your turn?"

"My turn," Ben happily agreed.

"What do you want to do?"

"You can lie on your back."

Dale thought that was a great idea and rolled over onto his back. "What now?"

"I'm going to make you hot and hard again, then I'm going to ride you, cowboy."

"I'm a fireman, not a cowboy," Dale pointed out.

Ben scowled at him. "Then I'll slide up and down your pole."

Dale chuckled, stroking a hand down Ben's spine until he reached his arse, covered with a fine layer of fuzz. He cupped it, letting his fingers stray toward the crack. Ben squirmed and Dale did it again, tracing the sensitive skin behind Ben's balls.

"Fuck!" Ben did a full-body shiver and sat up. His cock was almost purple, and it wouldn't take much to make him blow.

Ben reached into the basket and got the lube and condom. "Get me ready?"

"Don't tell me Mrs. Wilson packed the essentials?" Dale cracked up at Ben's disgusted face.

"Don't go there," Ben begged.

Dale flicked open the lube. Ben leaned over him to grab another cushion. His stiff cock dangled invitingly in front of Dale's mouth, but when Dale went to lick it, Ben jerked back.

"Don't! So close."

Dale had visions of Ben jerking off over his face, and fuck, didn't his prick stiffen at the thought? But he slicked his fingers and pressed one against Ben's hole. It took very little persuasion to enter and feel Ben's channel close around him. He fucked him gently, then pressed in another one. Dale made no attempt to go near Ben's prostate, knowing it would probably be game over if he brushed it.

"'Kay now," Ben said, his voice tight and hoarse. "Going to ride you now."

Dale withdrew his fingers and wiped them on the sheet. He reached for the condom, but Ben took it. Ben slicked his hand and jacked Dale's cock until it was hard and ready to go again; then he rolled the rubber down the hard shaft.

Ben positioned himself and slowly sank onto Dale's cock, his eyes closing as he concentrated. Dale saw his lips moving and smiled, knowing Ben was trying to stave off his orgasm. Eventually Ben was seated as far as he could go.

Another minute and Ben opened his eyes. He smiled down at Dale. "Ready to slide, fireman?"

"The bell is ringing," Dale said. "The engine is revved up and ready to go." Dale held Ben's hips, but that was the only control he had. This was Ben's ride, and he wasn't going to take long.

Ben rose up and gave him a strained smile. "Hold on tight." He was beautiful, wild and abandoned, none of the English gentleman as he fucked himself to completion. Sweat beaded across his forehead, and a blush spread up his torso.

Dale watched as Ben rode his cock, not wanting to take his eyes off him for a second. Ben's pace faltered and he slammed down one more time before he came, his cock untouched by either of them, striping come across Dale's belly and chest. Dale waited until Ben's eyes focused; then he moved, turning Ben on his back and fucking him until he came a second time.

They took time to recover, facing each other in the mess of the cushions. Dale kept his hand on Ben's hip, needing to keep him close. Ben buried his face against Dale's chest and stayed there, his breathing slowing down until Dale wondered if he was asleep. The rumbling sound of Dale's stomach made Ben raise his head, a broad grin on his face.

"Does the beast need feeding again?"

Dale's stomach growled again in agreement. "Is there any food left?"

"Mrs. Wilson packed for seconds."

As they ate more food, Ben said, "You know, I've always had a thing for firemen."

Dale grinned. It wasn't the first time he'd heard that. "Don't tell me, it's the sexy uniform."

"I prefer you out of uniform and standing to attention."

Dale snorted and tugged Ben against his chest and kissed him until they were both breathless. "You can slide down my pole anytime you want, your lordship."

Chapter Fourteen

BEN thrust his hands in his pockets and stamped his feet in a vain attempt to keep warm. Two days after their picnic, the temperature dropped again. There had been snowflakes—*snowflakes!*—overnight. Ben wished he was anywhere but standing on the village green watching football—Calminster village versus the fire station. It happened every year, but usually Ben managed to avoid having to watch the match. The organizer of the match, the local vicar, always invited him, but Ben had always refused politely, and neither acknowledged the fact that Ben would rather have hot pokers inserted into his eyes. Dale suggested he join in this year, but even he took a step back when Ben told him what he'd do if he mentioned it again. But Ben was a Boyfriend™, and that apparently meant freezing his nuts as he watched Dale run around the village green, getting muddier by the second and apparently enjoying every moment of it.

Everyone had looked surprised when Ben turned up. Ben was more surprised than all of them, but Dale insisted and Ben didn't want to upset him. He had no idea what was happening on the pitch, but from the yelling and hollering, the fire station's team was winning.

Ben stood on the sidelines, as usual slightly apart from everyone else. To his surprise, Mick's wife, Beth, smiled as she approached him, a small kid hanging on to each hand.

"Hello, Lord Calminster. Can we stand with you?"

He smiled at her a little shyly, unused to people seeking out his company just to be nice. "Please do. Who are these two?" He indicated the children, who hid behind her skirt.

"These are my grandchildren. James and Laura. Their parents are house-hunting, so we've got them for the day."

"Is Mick playing?" He hadn't seen Mick on the pitch.

"Not if he can help it. He's the sub, but they're under orders not to make him play." She grinned at him. "Who are you supporting?"

"Er… is it wrong if I say both?"

"Whatever you say is wrong?"

"Something like that." Ben rubbed his arms. He was going to be an icicle by the end of ninety minutes.

Beth smirked as she watched Dale tear down one side after the ball. "I can't believe he got you here."

"Nor can I. It wasn't by choice, believe me."

Dale shouted something and passed the ball. Ben watched his face the whole time, feeding off his enthusiasm and fun. Dale looked up and caught Ben's eye just for a second; then his attention was back on the pitch.

"He likes you being here for him. They all like their wives and partners here," Beth said. "They know no one wants to be here, and that's why it's special. Because everyone is making the effort."

Ben hadn't thought about the fact that no one wanted to be standing here getting cold. "At least it's only once a year."

She burst out laughing. "Once a year? You really are out of it, Lord Calminster. They get together as often as they can." She patted him on the arm at the horror on his face. "You win big brownie points for this."

"You mean he owes me?" Ben liked that idea.

"Now you get the idea."

Dale jogged up to him. "Hey. Hi, Beth."

Beth smiled at him. "Hi, Dale. I'll leave you two to chat."

"Having fun?" Dale beamed at Ben.

Ben took a deep breath. "Of course I am."

"Liar!"

"If you know I'm lying, why did you ask?"

"Just to see you squirm." Dale smirked at him.

"Is it over yet?"

"This is halftime."

Ben was in Special Hell. "You know I'm going to make you suffer."

"Bring it on!"

They stared at each other, and Ben knew Dale wanted to kiss him, but not here, not in front of the village.

"Maloney! Get your arse over here!" Tank's bellow interrupted their moment.

"I've got to—" Dale started.

Ben nodded. "Later."

After another half an hour, Ben was convinced he'd never be warm again. He was about to escape to the café when Patrick, the young waiter, and his mother approached.

"Hi, Patrick. What can I do for you?"

Patrick gave his mother a grim nod, then took a couple of steps closer. "We're so sorry, your lordship. We had no idea."

"No idea about what?" Ben knew he was fuzzy from the cold, but he didn't have a clue what Patrick was talking about. "Patrick, what's happened?"

"It's Uncle Olly. He's been the one starting the fires," Patrick's expression clearly expected the worst. Ben stared at him. "Olly? Oliver Miller?" The man he'd sacked a few weeks ago.

Tears spilled over onto Mrs. Rayham's cheeks as Patrick nodded. "He's my brother," she said.

"He started all the fires?" Ben wasn't surprised. Miller had a vicious streak in him a mile wide.

"He's so angry at you because his wife has left him and taken the kids after he got sacked. He just wanted to cause some trouble."

"By hurting his friends in the village?" Ben scowled at them, and Mrs. Rayham shrank back.

"He wasn't thinking right, your lordship. When he realized he'd killed Bonnie, he was right upset."

"Where is he now?" Ben asked.

"We don't know," Patrick said. "I made Mum call PC Verne when we found petrol cans in our shed. But he's been missing a couple of days."

Ben nodded. "Let me know if you see him. And thank you for telling me."

Mrs. Rayham wiped her cheeks. "He's a good man."

Ben pressed his lips together to hold back the angry words, but Patrick got there first.

"No, he isn't, Mum. I know he's your brother, but he's always been vile and too quick with his fists. Cath and the kids are better away from him."

"Don't say such things," she said, but Patrick stood resolute.

"You said it yourself, Mum. Aunty Cath needs to make a new life." Patrick held out his hand to Ben. "I won't let him hurt anyone else."

Ben shook his hand, impressed by the young man. "Make an appointment to see me next week, Patrick."

Patrick looked surprised, but he nodded. "Come on, Mum. We promised to help with the teas."

They headed for the café. Ben caught Dale's worried expression. He smiled, and Dale smiled back and focused on his game again.

Ben made a note to call Verne if he didn't get frostbite. Hell, he'd tap out the phone number with his nose if it got Miller locked up.

LATER that day, when Ben was warmer and Dale had stopped laughing at his complaints, he worked at his desk while Dale sat in the armchair by the fire, reading the latest Jack Reacher novel. He'd spoken to PC Verne and Station Commander Fang about Miller. Neither of them were surprised at Ben's revelations.

"Ms. Barrett, your lordship."

Ben frowned as his new lawyer swept in, as immaculate as ever. "Sabrina, what are you doing here?"

"Good afternoon, Ben. I thought I'd keep you up-to-date with my father's antics." She smiled at Dale. "And meet my replacement."

Dale got to his feet and held out his hand. "Pleased to meet you."

"Delighted to meet you, Mr. Maloney." Sabrina arched her eyebrow. Ben thought she wielded them like a lethal weapon. "I gave up waiting for Ben to introduce us."

"Likewise. I think he was afraid of what might happen."

Ben groaned and thunked his forehead on his desk. Sabrina and Dale both laughed at him, and Ben knew he was in deep trouble.

Colson came in with afternoon tea. Ben was tempted to escape with him as he left, because Sabrina and Dale were having far too much fun at his expense.

But Sabrina took her teacup and looked at them both. "I think we need to get down to work, gentlemen. I'm not just here to see Ben squirm."

"I told your father *again* that it'll be a cold day in hell before he gets his hands on Calminster Hall," Ben said. "He doesn't seem to be listening. He has a controlling share in Calminster Enterprises, and now he's called for a board meeting of Calminster Enterprises for Monday morning to force the merger through." The last part was mainly for Dale's benefit, as Ben hadn't told him that.

Dale's expression darkened. "He can do that?"

Sabrina nodded. "As a major shareholder, he can force a vote of no confidence in Lord Calminster and force the takeover through."

Ben's stomach had not stopped churning since Sabrina told him that. Nevertheless, he waited as calmly as he could for Sabrina's response.

"After our last conversation, I've spoken to all the major shareholders."

"And?"

"They are all behind you, Ben. Every last one of them. Barrett cannot force this takeover."

"But he has a controlling interest!" Ben said.

"On the contrary, he *had* a controlling interest. He sold me a fifteen percent stake in Calminster Enterprises as a birthday present. I sold it to Freely & Sons before I resigned, giving them the majority shareholding. The takeover is a dead duck."

"You didn't think to tell me this earlier?" Ben asked.

"It might not have worked. Freely likes you, but business is business."

Sabrina smiled so coldly, Ben felt the short hairs shrivel on his balls. "I have reorganized Calminster Enterprises. We'll see what happens at the meeting on Monday, where I'm proposing Calminster takes over Barrett Media and Leisure."

"Your father—"

"Don't worry, we only want Media and Leisure. We'll leave the smaller companies for him to tinker with."

"Have you had any sleep?" Ben asked, still processing her words.

"You don't pay me to sleep," she said, plucking an imaginary thread from her skirt.

"Thank God for Freely."

"He would have bought the shares just to annoy my father. They have history. He would pay to see my father ground into the dirt."

"You knew about this history beforehand?"

It was a rhetorical question, but she chose to answer him anyway. "I know everything, Ben."

Ben made a mental note for the hundredth time never to underestimate this woman. "Can we really take over your father's company?"

"I doubt it. But it'll be fun trying."

"You're a very scary woman, Sabrina Barrett."

"Sabrina Bradshaw," she corrected, getting to her feet. "It's time I left the Barrett name behind."

Ben inclined his head. "Ms. Bradshaw."

"Lord Calminster." Sabrina smirked and bent to kiss Ben. "I need to get back to the office and minimize the damage my father's bound to attempt."

Ben hugged her with more feeling than he'd had the whole time they were together. She allowed it for a moment and then stepped back. "That's enough of that. It's not appropriate for our working relationship."

"I'm starting to wonder who is working for whom."

"Best not to think about it too much. Your head might start hurting. Good to meet you, Dale." With that she left.

Ben shook his head and breathed much easier when the front door had shut behind her.

"She's one scary broad," Dale observed, speaking for the first time.

"More scary than Barrett?"

"He's just a bully. I've seen a million dudes like him. I don't see many women like Sabrina."

Ben gritted his teeth. "Does she turn you on?"

Dale raised an eyebrow. "Uh… gay, like you?"

"Just ignore me. I'm being a moron."

"She doesn't do a thing for me. I like men like you." Dale stepped into Ben's space. "I like you."

Ben rested his head on Dale's shoulder, his hands lightly on Dale's hips. "I'll get the dungeons ready for Thomas Barrett."

"You do that. Have you got a rack?"

"Didn't you see the torture room?"

Dale stared at him, wide-eyed and excited. "No way, you've got a torture room? Show it to me now."

Ben raised his head. "Seriously?"

"Hell, yeah." Dale grinned like a kid in a sweetie shop.

"Come on, then. But if you piss me off, I'll put you in the stocks."

Dale's eyes went dark. "I can think of other uses for the stocks."

Ben smacked him on the arm. "You're a kinky bastard."

"Well, duh!"

Chapter Fifteen

THE May Day parade had gone without a hitch, and the pole stayed upright despite the Calminster fire crew's prediction that it would topple during the dance. Dale endured several days of bets being left on the whiteboard on how long it would take to fall over. Dale rolled his eyes and let them cackle it out, knowing any sign of weakness on his part would be pounced on immediately. Still, he was relieved when it was all over. Perhaps now they'd stop leaving L-plates on his locker. When they stuck one on the maypole, Dale stopped being so optimistic.

Dale spent two hours lifting kids in and out of the fire engine, letting them play with the siren and the horn, and generally behaving like a big kid himself. It was fun, but after a while his back started to ache, and he needed a replacement mug.

"Time out," he called to two of the firemen chatting close by.

To his relief, Keith looked over and nodded. "My turn."

Dale said goodbye to the kids and parents waiting in line and walked over to Tank. He groaned as he rolled his shoulders. "Damn, some of those kids are heavy."

Tank snorted. "Why do you think we let the newbie volunteer?"

"Thanks." Dale groaned. "You could've warned me."

"Where's the fun in that?"

Dale resisted the urge to thump his boss. "Have you seen anything out of the ordinary?"

Tank shook his head. They were all on the alert for Miller and/or suspicious behavior. The small fires had died down over the past few days as the village prepared for the parade. After the meeting, the parade organizers had insisted every teenager get involved in helping whether they wanted to or not. However, they all knew with everyone's attention diverted, the parade day was prime time to set another fire.

"You giving your boy a show?" Tank asked.

Midway through a shoulder roll, Dale froze. "What do you mean?" He followed Tank's gaze. Ben was with a small group of people, but his attention was focused on Dale until he caught Dale's eye and flushed, turning away.

Tank rolled his eyes. "You two are going to have to be a damn sight more subtle if you're supposed to be keeping it quiet."

Dale frowned at him. "What are we keeping quiet?"

"You and his lordship, sitting in the tree, k-i-s-s-i-n-g?"

Firstly, he hadn't done nearly enough kissing with Ben. He was convinced there would never be enough kissing with Ben. Secondly, he hadn't realized their relationship was still supposed to be a secret. It wasn't like half the village didn't know already. Dale hadn't moved halfway across the country to be shoved back in the closet. Then he saw the worried frown on Ben's face. They were going to have a talk, and soon. But first he needed a can of something cold and fizzy and a burger. Christ, he was starving.

He nodded at Ben, hoping that would reassure him. The frown on Ben's face eased a little, and he nodded back. Dale also noticed the curious glances from Ben's companions. Tank was right. If Ben was trying to keep his interest in Dale quiet, he was failing miserably.

Dale looked at Tank. "Okay if I take a break? I need food. I can take an order for all of you."

Tank clapped him on the back, nearly driving Dale to his knees. "Now you're talking. Take Mick with you. He needs the exercise." He raised his voice so Mick could hear him.

"You've got to stop doing that," Dale grumbled as he got to his feet, brushing the dirt off his knees.

Mick joined Dale and Tank. "'Bout fuckin' time. Thought you were gonna starve me."

Dale snorted as Mick patted his rounded belly. Mick certainly didn't look starved. His wife, Beth, believed in good food piled high. Sometimes Mick would bring in her meals for the crew, who worshipped the ground she walked on. Dale and Mick took orders and headed to the catering area, where the barbecue and the beer tent were set up.

"How're you doing, Dale?" Mick asked out of the blue.

"I'm fine. Why?" Dale was startled by the question.

"I always keep an eye on the newbies," Mick said. "We've been so busy, I haven't got around to asking the question."

"You're a good bloke, Mick."

"I know," Mick said wryly. "I'm well trained by Beth."

"She's the best. You're so lucky."

"You think I don't know it? You haven't answered my question."

Dale thought about it for a moment before giving a snap answer. "I'm really happy, Mick. Making the move to Calminster was the best decision ever."

"I'm really glad," Mick said. "You've fitted in well. Even the commander likes you, and I thought that was an impossibility after you pranged Bertha." He squinted at the beer tent. "I could murder a pint."

"Later," Dale said as they dodged a small group of people.

Mick shook his head. "Not 'til tomorrow evening. I'm picking up an early shift for Lola. She's still dealing with stuff after her mum died."

"I didn't know." He'd said hello in passing to the guys on the other shifts, but that was all. "You tell her that I'll help with any shifts if she needs me to."

"Great. I will."

The queue for the barbecue was long, but it gave Dale a chance to study Ben as unobtrusively as he could, although when he caught Mick rolling his eyes, he realized maybe he wasn't as subtle as he thought.

By this time they reached the front of the line, and a woman wielding a wicked pair of tongs smiled at them.

"What do you want, gents?"

Mick beamed at her. "Sharon, darl, we've got a long order."

The people behind Mick and Dale groaned, but Sharon just nodded. "Let's start."

THEY walked away fifteen minutes later with boxes full of food and drink, the aromas making Dale's stomach rumble.

Dale drooled at the large quantity of food in the box. "That was quick."

Mick grunted and carefully held on to his box as he scratched his nose. "The women doing the cooking are the cooks for the local school. They do the barbecue every year because they're used to cooking for large numbers."

"Wish they cooked for us," Dale said. "No, I wish your Beth cooked for us, but these ladies run a close second."

"I worship every hair on their furry chins."

Dale snorted out a laugh. Then his attention was diverted as he spotted an elegantly dressed woman hanging on to Ben's arm. "Who's the woman with Ben?"

"Karen something-or-other. She's some sort of celebrity," Mick said. "Been on TV once or twice. I dunno. Ask Keith. He's more likely to know."

"'Kay."

Karen Something-or-Other was too bloody comfortable on Ben's arm in Dale's opinion. Then Ben looked around, his gaze growing heated when it landed on him, and Dale realized he was being an idiot. She was probably a friend or something.

"Hurry up," Mick said. "The food'll be cold."

Dale tore his gaze away from Ben and hurried after Mick. He had to focus. Otherwise, he was going to make a right prat of himself.

"About bloody time," Tank grumbled as they approached. "Thought you two had run off with the money."

"Yeah, yeah, 'cos we'd get a long way with forty quid." Mick put down the box thankfully.

Tank swung the small boy down from the engine and smiled at the queue of families waiting their turn. "Time for our lunch. We'll be back soon." He knelt in front of one young child, his chin wobbling as if he was about to cry. "We won't be long, Jimmy. I promise."

"Do you know everyone here?" Dale asked.

"More or less," Tank said before he stuffed half his burger in his mouth.

Dale couldn't imagine only ever living in one place. He'd never lived in one place for more than three years, even as a kid.

"You know Tank and his lordship went to the same school?" Mick said.

Dale blinked at Tank. "You did? You didn't tell me."

"Not my business, mate. Besides, we weren't friends or anything. Poor bloke. He wasn't really friends with anyone. Everyone was too scared of his dad and stayed away from him."

"Jeez," Dale breathed out. He wanted to rush over to Ben, wrap him up in a bear hug, and tell him it would be all right.

Tank turned away from Dale's accusing eyes. "You've got to understand; the old lord was a bit of a dick."

"But Ben was a kid."

"And his dad could make trouble for any of us. Most of the parents worked on the estate or in the village. It wasn't just their jobs; most of them lived in a house provided by the estate."

Dale took a deep breath and tried to smile at Tank. It was all a long time ago, and he didn't know any of them then. He just felt so sorry for Ben. No wonder he was screwed up about relationships.

"You've got it bad for him, then?" Keith asked.

"Yeah." Dale didn't hesitate. Someone had to have Ben's back. He waited, but Keith just made a grunt. It sounded satisfied, but he didn't say anything.

"Are you going to stand around, or are you doing your job?"

They all turned to see a grumpy and harassed-looking man with three kids around his knees.

Dale opened his mouth to point out this was not his fucking job, but he caught Tank shaking his head, and he shut it again.

"Afternoon, Frank. Hey, monsters, have you got a hug for your uncle Tank?" He knelt down, and the two boys rushed to hug him. The third boy, obviously younger than the other two, hid behind his father's legs.

Dale stared at Tank and then the grumpy git, noting the similarities in their facial features. "This is your brother?"

"For my sins. Dale, meet Frank and my nephews, Alfie, Mushroom's the one hiding, and Tom is the ginger."

Dale frowned. "Mushroom?"

"When he was born, he had a head like a mushroom," Tank said.

"He didn't." Frank shoved his brother. "Tank just likes giving kids stupid nicknames. This is Kit."

Kit was obviously tired since he sucked his thumb. He was also clutching a stuffed toy tightly to his chest. Dale got down on his haunches and smiled at the little boy.

"Hey, Kit. I like your bear. Does he have a name?"

The little boy hesitated, then said, "He's called Ted."

"Hello, Ted," Dale said solemnly. "Would you like to go on the engine?"

Kit nodded. "He says yes."

Dale got to his feet and held out his hand. "Come on, then." He led Kit to the engine, Kit's brothers following behind. There was a rumbling of discontent from people at the head of the queue. Dale sent them an apologetic smile and said, "Just five minutes."

"They've been on the engine hundreds of times," Frank said, "but every time they see Tank, you'd think they'd never seen a fire engine before."

Frank and his kids had their turn, and then Dale and Tank spent another hour manning the never-ending line of parents and their children, wanting to play on the engine. After a group of teen girls that Dale recognized as the dancers from the maypole declared it was their turn, and spent ten minutes trying to flirt with Dale, he begged Tank for another break.

"Mick and Keith can do the last couple of hours," Tank said.

It hadn't escaped Dale's notice that Mick had avoided any contact with the children thus far. Mick grumbled, but at Tank's scowl, he subsided and took Dale's place, much to the disgust of the girls, who obviously didn't appreciate Mick's older charms.

Dale spent ten minutes searching for Ben. When he eventually found him talking to Mrs. Manning, Dale claimed he absolutely had to talk to Ben. She let them go with a knowing smile. Dale led Ben behind the tents, and before Ben could say a word, Dale tugged him into his arms and kissed him. Ben stiffened, his arms flailing as he tried to pull away, but Dale wouldn't let him go.

"What the hell? We can't. Here."

Dale ignored Ben's protests and kissed him again. Finally, Ben relaxed a fraction. Dale grunted in satisfaction and hauled Ben closer, one hand tangled in his hair and the other cupping his ass. Ben curled his fingers against Dale's chest, submitting to Dale's onslaught. Dale kept kissing Ben until the tension left his muscles. The need for air paramount, Dale raised his head, noticing with satisfaction Ben's glazed eyes and swollen lips.

Ben ran his tongue along his bottom lip. "You make me do dangerous things."

"Kissing me is dangerous?"

"Being within ten feet of you is dangerous."

Yes, Dale was smug about that. He knew the effect he had on Ben, but then, Ben had the same effect on him.

"I just need to be careful. The villagers—"

"I hate to be the one to break it to you, your lordship," Dale said carefully, "but the whole village knows you're gay."

Ben stared at him. "They do?"

They both swung around at the cough. Mrs. Manning smiled uncomfortably. "I'm sorry to interrupt, Bene… Lord Calminster, but you're expected…." She waved at the stage.

"Oh, oh, yes." Ben visibly got himself together.

Dale was about to say something when Mrs. Manning spoke first. "No one cares about—you know."

"You know?" Ben asked.

"The fact you're—er—gay. The village just wants you to be happy." Mrs. Manning stumbled over the words but she was obviously sincere. For his part, Ben was wide-eyed and looked as if he wanted to be anywhere but having this conversation.

Dale grinned at Mrs. Manning, making a mental note to find a quiet corner and hug the woman senseless. He slung his arm around Ben's shoulders and tugged him close. "He's going to be happy. I'm going to make sure of it." He winked conspiratorially at Mrs. Manning.

Ben scowled, but he stayed tucked into Dale's side.

"Er—speeches, Lord Calminster?" Mrs. Manning's smile was apologetic.

Dale squeezed Ben's shoulder. "Go on. I'll see you later."

Ben followed Mrs. Manning a couple of steps and then turned back to Dale. "Will you be here?"

"If I don't get called away, I'll be here," Dale promised. Wild horses wouldn't drag him away, but a callout was something different. He prayed Olly Miller would get drunk and take the day off.

Ben stared at him, obviously seeking reassurance. Dale smiled and leaned back against the fire engine, showing Ben he wasn't moving from the spot. Ben smiled back.

"Lord Calminster?" Mrs. Manning sounded a little more impatient this time.

Dale flapped his hands, telling Ben to move on. Ben turned back to Mrs. Manning and apologized. As Ben walked away, Dale wondered how he could be so lucky. The man obviously wanted him and, more to the point, needed him. Dale was going to spend as much time as he could showing Ben just how important he was.

Chapter Sixteen

AS was his usual habit, Ben left the parade soon after the speeches. It gave the villagers the chance to relax without feeling he was judging them. He'd been aware of Dale's hot gaze on him as he gave out the prizes. Unfortunately, the fire crew had to leave before he got a chance to speak to Dale, but he'd left a text on Ben's phone, saying he'd be over later that night.

Ben walked back to the house to be greeted by the dogs, pleased that their master was finally home. Fluffy and Fern stuck wet noses in his eyes and Frankie wriggled in ecstasy. The house was empty, the staff having the day off for the parade. Ben kicked off his shoes, poured himself a large brandy, and crashed on his sofa, surrounded by the dogs. This was one day of the year he allowed himself an afternoon off.

It was only once he'd relaxed, the warmth of the brandy seeping through him, that he realized how much tension he'd been carrying all day. Ben had been expecting trouble, a fire somewhere, but it seemed Olly Miller had decided to take the day off, like everyone else. Ben was relieved. Every time the Hall received a call that there was a fire, Ben worried. He knew they'd all been minor, poor Bonnie aside, but nevertheless Dale was on the front line—his man. Ben knew he was going to have to get used to that if they were going to stay together.

Ben took another sip of brandy and switched on the TV. He flicked through the channels trying to find something to watch. "Five hundred channels of bloody nothing," he muttered.

His phone saved him from tedium. Sabrina's beautiful face filled his screen. Ben hesitated for a moment, and then he answered. "Sabrina?"

"Ben?" She sounded distracted.

"Who did you expect it to be?"

"I'd have been happy if it was your caveman."

"Caveman? Sabrina, are you drunk?"

"Caveman, fireman, it's the same thing."

"If you say so." Personally Ben was quite content with his fireman.

"Have you heard from my father?"

"Not since the shareholders meeting."

The meeting had been explosive, but Ben had come out with a vote of confidence and his company intact.

"He's still trying to cause trouble."

Ben sighed and took a large swallow of brandy. "We knew he was going to. I'd better talk to Freely again."

Sabrina huffed in his ear. "I've already talked to them all again."

"Why didn't we have this conversation before I decided to go into business with your father?" Ben could have saved himself a lot of hassle and a relationship he didn't want.

"It's not my fault if you decided to underestimate me," she said lightly.

"I had no idea—"

"And that's just the way I like it."

"Did you ring up just to gloat?"

"Yes."

Ben rolled his eyes because Sabrina was never going to change. "Bye, Sabrina."

"Bye, Ben."

Ben disconnected the call, then finished his brandy and closed his eyes. He could do with a nap. He jumped out of his skin when someone knocked at the study door.

"Hello?"

Colson peered around the door. "Would you like some tea?"

"What are you doing here?" Ben asked. "You've got the day off."

Colson came into the room with a tray. "They needed more cake. Mrs. Wilson sent me to get some. Then she rang me to say they'd found the cakes behind the beer barrels."

Ben frowned. "Is that supposed to make sense?"

"It's Mrs. Wilson," Colson said as if that explained it all. "Anyway, I realized you were home, and I thought you might want a cup of tea."

"Yes, please." Ben accepted the cup from Colson. "Are you going back to the parade?"

Colson shook his head so vigorously Ben was sure it was going to fall off. "I'm going to hide."

The Fireman's Pole

"Stay for a while?" Ben indicated the armchair.

"Of course." Colson sat down and leaned back in his chair. He sighed and crossed his ankles.

"Why've you never left the Hall?" Ben asked.

"You've never asked me that question before."

"I never thought about it. You were just always here. Like Mrs. Wilson."

"Ah. And now she's not here, you're worrying about me leaving?"

Colson always had the ability to see right through Ben.

Ben shrugged. "Maybe, a little."

"I've never wanted to leave the Hall," Colson said. "I'm happy here. Dad was the butler, and he taught me everything."

"He trained you well."

Colson smiled a little sadly. "Yes, he did."

"But didn't you ever want to do something else?"

"I suppose, maybe once or twice. But once I met Joe, I knew I'd be here forever."

Ben choked on his tea. He spluttered and flailed out. Colson swiftly took Ben's cup out of his hand and handed him a tissue.

Ben wiped his mouth and took a moment to breathe before he said, "You and Joe? Joe, the head gardener?"

The huge barrel-chested gardener with an expletive for every other word?

Colson's lips twitched. "Do you know another Joe? You really had no idea?"

"Not a clue."

"You do know I'm gay?"

"I know about you, but you and Joe—why didn't you tell me?"

Colson poured out more tea. "Try not to choke on this one, sir."

"How long have you been together?"

"Twenty-five years. I was seventeen."

Ben sipped at his drink and tried not to feel envious at the thought of Colson and Joe's relationship.

"Joe doesn't like anyone gossiping about him," Colson said. "I don't mind who knows, but he's a very private person."

"So you've spent all this time in the closet?"

Colson shrugged. "I love him. Besides, it's not like people don't know we share a home. I just let Joe think no one knows. It makes him happy, and I'd do anything to make him happy."

"Why, Mr. Colson, you are very devious." Ben knew they shared a cottage; why had he never joined the dots?

Colson smirked at him over the rim of the teacup. "Yes, your lordship. I like to think so."

The smile slipped off Ben's face. "Everyone knows about me too."

"Does that bother you?" Colson asked.

"A little," Ben admitted. "I thought I'd managed to be discreet."

"I think you were," Colson said carefully.

"Were?"

"Before…."

Ben gave a wry smile as Colson hesitated. "Before Dale?"

"Yes."

"He's different."

"He makes you happy."

Ben nodded. "Is it too soon?"

"To be happy?" Colson asked. "Is there supposed to be a time frame?"

"How long for you and Joe?"

"About fifteen minutes. Give or take ten minutes." Colson pulled out his wallet and handed over a picture of two men, their arms around each other. They were laughing and staring into each other's eyes. Ben recognized Colson immediately, but Joe was a shock. Ben couldn't remember Joe being that young and carefree. "This is the day we met."

"I wish I'd known," Ben said.

"Don't tell Joe. He's still under the illusion you think he's a confirmed bachelor."

Ben snorted. "Up to five minutes ago, that was the case."

"This may be presumptuous, Mr. Ben, but I'm glad you met Mr. Maloney."

"You didn't like Sabrina." Ben didn't even bother to phrase it as a question.

"Ms. Barrett didn't make you happy like Mr. Maloney does."

"I thought I could marry her."

Colson nodded, and Ben felt he was holding back on what he really wanted to say.

"You can say it."

"It's never a good idea to marry for business."

Ben sighed. "I knew it. I just didn't want to admit it. So you like Dale?"

"He rescued Mrs. Wilson. Of course I like him."

"He thinks you're hot!" The minute the words left his mouth, Ben wished he could've taken them back.

"I *am* hot," Colson said. Ben got the impression he was pleased and embarrassed at the same time.

"And modest."

"That too." Colson got to his feet and placed the cups on the tray. "I'm going to find Joe. He's hiding somewhere in the garden. Do you want me to get you some dinner?"

Ben shook his head. "I'm having dinner with Dale tonight."

"In that case, I'll see you in the morning. Good night, Mr. Ben."

"Good night, Harry."

Colson raised his eyes at the unusual use of his first name, but he said nothing as he left the study.

Ben shook his head as he thought about Colson and Joe. They'd spent their lives hiding their relationship. He could understand living like that; he knew plenty of men in his social and business circles who conducted discreet relationships with each other. But Dale was different. Ben already knew Dale hated hiding his relationship with Baz. He couldn't ask Dale to step back into the closet again.

He yawned and closed his eyes. Then his phone started ringing. "Bloody hell, can't I have five minutes? Yes?"

"Is this a bad time?"

Ben's irritated mood vanished at the sound of Dale's voice. "Not for you. It's just been busy."

"Are you still at the fair?"

"I'm in my study. Hiding."

Dale chuckled. "Not very well, if everyone keeps finding you."

"I was never any good at hide-and-seek."

"Of course you aren't. They even find you in the dark corners."

"Perhaps you can help me?" Ben suggested.

"Play hide-and-seek?"

"I was thinking more the hide, less the seek."

"Sounds good to me, babe. How about hiding in my cottage?" Dale sounded as exhausted as Ben felt.

"What time do you want me there?"

"About eight."

Ben yawned, and he heard Dale's answering yawn.

"Don't do that," Dale scolded. "I'm having a hard enough time staying awake as it is."

"I'm going to have a nap," Ben said, not remotely repentant.

"Bastard!"

"I know!" Ben was happy to be very smug. "Have there been any callouts?"

"Not yet, but it's early in the day."

"Fingers crossed it stays that way."

"Me too, Ben. Uh… I've got to go. The commander's calling a meeting."

"Okay. See you at your place."

Ben scowled at the phone after Dale said goodbye. Fuck it, he needed a nap. He turned off the ringer and stretched out on the sofa. If anyone needed him, they could bloody well wait until later.

AT eight o'clock precisely, Ben pushed open the gate of Dale's cottage, a bottle of merlot in his hand. The smile of anticipation slipped from his face when he saw a man at the door talking to Dale. Ben knew who it was. Dale had shown him a photo of his ex-boyfriend. For a split second, Ben felt like bolting; then he took a deep breath and walked up the path in time to hear Baz's "Hey, babe."

"What are you doing here?" Dale made no move to let Baz into the cottage. From the scowl on his face, he didn't seem pleased to see Baz, who was also holding a bottle of wine. Ben was pleased to see his wine was better.

Baz seemed to realize Dale's lack of enthusiasm for his sudden appearance. "Aren't you pleased to see me?"

"No," Dale said flatly.

"Aw, come on, Dale. Invite me in. We can drink the wine and talk."

Then Dale spotted Ben and he smiled, pushing past Baz to join Ben. "Hey," Dale kissed him on the cheek.

Ben forced a smile on his face. "You've got a guest. I can come back another time."

Dale grabbed Ben's hand. "You're the guest. Baz is just going."

"Are you sure?"

"I didn't invite him."

"Are you sure you don't want to talk to him?" Ben knew Dale had been devastated at Baz's betrayal. If they had things to discuss…. "We can always make this another night."

"Fuck that," Dale said succinctly. "Give me a minute and he'll be gone."

Dale put his arm around Ben's shoulders and turned to where Baz waited, the cheesy grin gone and a frown on his face. "Ben, this is Baz, my ex. Baz, this is Lord Calminster." He was not giving his ex-boyfriend permission to be friendly. "We've got dinner plans, so now's not convenient. Give me a call next time."

Baz looked incredulous that Dale expected him to leave. "I've driven all the way here."

Dale shrugged. "You should've rung first. I'm busy."

"You didn't wait long to replace me," Baz said snidely.

"At least I waited until I was out of the relationship," Dale snapped, and Ben felt the shudder that went through him. "'Bye, Baz."

Dale pushed Ben through the front and shut the front door. "Go through to the kitchen," he said to Ben. They both jumped as Baz thumped the front door in anger. But then they heard him stomping down the path and the gate slamming shut. Dale forced a smile for Ben. "Thank Christ for that. He's got the message. Sorry about that. Baz never was known for his sense of timing."

Ben moved, pushing Dale up against the wall, and kissed him with a fierce intensity. Taken by surprise at the sudden onslaught, Dale parted his lips, and Ben thrust his tongue in, exploring Dale's mouth. He rested his hands on Dale's hips, his fingers biting in almost painfully. Even though Dale had made it obvious he didn't want Baz there, his sudden appearance rattled Ben. Their relationship was still so new, he needed to do something, had to stake his claim, and from the way Dale opened up, he seemed more than happy to let Ben get all toppy.

Eventually Ben pulled back and stared at Dale. He licked his lips before he said, "He's not having you again."

"I don't want him."

"Are you sure about that?"

Dale cupped Ben's jaw and fixed him with his gaze. "I am sure. Baz had his time and fucked it up. I'm only interested in you."

Ben nodded once and tried to step back, but Dale caught him by the hips and pressed them together. The kiss might have started in anger and jealousy, but now they were both turned on. Dale pressed his arousal against the mound in Ben's jeans.

Ben hissed, and his eyes grew darker. "Dinner. Can it wait?"

"Yeah, it's only a beef stew and it's in the slow cooker."

Ben wasn't interested in the menu, just if it could wait the time it took for Dale to fuck him through the mattress. "Your bedroom, now."

Dale led Ben up the stairs and into his bedroom. The duvet was turned back, and in pride of place on the bedside table, there were lube and condoms. Ben could have called him on it, but he was more interested in getting Dale naked and spread out, ready for him to feast on. He'd spent all day watching Dale from afar, unable to talk to him, let alone touch him. Now the ex had been dismissed, there weren't any staff to interrupt them, and Ben wanted to rub up against Dale and remind Dale who he belonged to. He slipped his hands under Dale's T-shirt, reveling in the feel of warm skin and soft hair.

"You don't have anything to prove," Dale said unexpectedly, his words breaking the silence in the room.

"Huh?" Ben stared at him, confused.

"You don't have anything to prove, Ben. Baz is in my past. You are my present."

"And the future?" It came out more of a challenge than Ben expected.

Dale picked up one of Ben's hands and licked across the inside of his wrist. *Bastard!* How did he know doing that was guaranteed to make Ben's knees wobbly? Dale picked up his other wrist and did it again. The anger and aggression from Baz's appearance faded away. This wasn't a boardroom deal; their merger had been signed, sealed, and delivered from the first moment Ben caught a glimpse of that tantalizing furred belly.

"And the future," Dale said and leaned in for a kiss.

Ben had never had a partner who loved kissing as much as Dale. On the other hand, he'd never wanted to kiss anyone as much as Dale. He loved a hard masculine mouth with the roughness of scruff beneath.

Dale stopped kissing and breathed into Ben's mouth. He slid his hands down Ben's torso and cupped his dick through his jeans. Ben groaned and shoved his groin into Dale's touch.

That was enough talking. Ben needed skin and action. A certain fireman had a pole and Ben was determined to slide down it. He kept one eye on the spider in the corner, though—just in case it decided to join in. He definitely didn't believe in threesomes.

Chapter Seventeen

THE shrill alarm sounded. Dale shoved in the last mouthful of cake and washed it down with tea, then headed for Bertha.

"Jesus, I hope Miller's not starting again," he muttered.

The police hadn't found Oliver Miller since the last fire.

Tank and Mick were already there, and they were huddled over the paper.

"Where's the shout?" Dale asked.

They turned to him, both pale and his stomach churned.

"What's the matter with you two? You both look like you've seen a ghost."

Tank waved the paper at him. "It's the shout."

"Yeah? Don't tell me my cottage is on fire."

He grinned at them, but Tank just shook his head.

"Not your place. It's Calminster Hall."

Dale felt the blood drain from his head.

"Don't you dare fucking pass out," Tank muttered. He pushed and shoved Dale into the cab and climbed in the driver's seat. For once Dale didn't protest at not taking the wheel. He knew he wasn't safe to focus on driving right now.

"Are you okay?" Mick asked, his expression sympathetic.

Dale was one breath away from a meltdown, so no, he wasn't okay, but he just muttered something incoherent and thankfully Mick left him alone.

As they raced down the drive to Calminster Hall, Dale could see thick black smoke pouring out from the right-hand side of the building.

"The commander's called for backup from Winchester," Tank said. "The police and ambulances are on their way."

"We're going to need all the help we can get," Mick agreed. "Any reports of casualties?"

"Not yet. The fire started in the servants' quarters. They're not sure how."

"*Fuck!*" Dale muttered, thinking of the elegant rooms being destroyed by the fire.

Tank gave him a hard stare. "You gonna hold it together?"

"Yep."

"Sure?"

Dale snapped a glance at him. "I'm a fucking professional. You know that."

Tank's lips twitched.

"Shut the fuck up," Dale said. He ignored the snorts from the others.

Tank pulled up in front of the house and jumped out. The staff huddled to one side, moving out of the way as the other appliances drove into the courtyard. Tank and Dale headed toward the small group. Dale could see Colson, Mrs. Wilson and Lisa; everyone except Ben. *Fuck!* Where the hell was Ben? Dale frantically searched the crowd, there was no sign of him.

The butler limped toward them, his face and hands soot-stained. "Thank you for getting here so quickly. We can't find Mr. Ben."

Fear pitted itself in Dale's stomach, but he kept his face as impassive as he could, knowing Tank wouldn't hesitate to make him stand down if he thought he would endanger the team.

Tank glanced at Dale before he said, "Is everyone else out?"

Mr. Colson's face grew pinched. "Everyone except his lordship. He was going to take the dogs for a walk, but we found them in the kitchen. The grounds staff are combing the gardens and parkland for him. We searched through as much of the house as we could before the smoke got too much."

"Where did the fire start?" Tank asked.

"We think in the boot room, but we don't know how. The security guards went through the house, but they didn't find him."

Tank snapped out orders to the crews, getting the appliances around the back. Before he could relegate Dale to the outside, Dale said, "I'm going to find him."

To give Tank credit, he didn't argue, but he gave Dale a firm "Stay in formation and don't fucking try anything stupid."

Dale gave one nod and focused on getting on his breathing apparatus. He was a fucking professional. He repeated it like a mantra to stop his head spinning off into la-la land.

They entered the house via the main hallway. The fire appeared to be contained to one side, the smoke minimal in the large empty space. Tank sent Dale's team along the east wing, and the other along the west wing. As they cleared room after room, the tension grew in Dale. The smoke got thicker, but the flames appeared to be contained downstairs. The large dining and reception rooms that were rarely used except for formal occasions were empty. Mick and Dale cleared them and then headed into the smaller rooms. Still empty. They cleared the whole wing and headed back to the hall, the other teams arriving back at the same time. They all shook their heads at Dale. Fear pitted itself in the base of Dale's stomach. Where the hell was Ben?

All the teams met back in the hall. The lord of the manor was still nowhere to be found. Then they headed downstairs, Dale and Mick taking one of the servant's staircases. Mick opened the door to one of the small rooms that served as a storage area.

"He's here!"

Was he still alive? Fear consumed Dale, but he couldn't afford to fall apart now. He had a job to do and that was to get Ben out of the house before the fire took hold. Dale rushed to kneel by Ben. He was lying facedown in one corner of the room. Dale carefully turned him over. Ben was unconscious, but Dale didn't have time to see if he was breathing or not. He hoisted Ben over his shoulder, headed out of the room, and up the stairs. Mick followed, hard on his heels.

The smoke was thicker than it had been before. As they exited through the ornate doors, Dale saw an ambulance had joined them. The paramedics rushed forward, and one of them tried to relieve Dale of his burden. Dale ignored them and laid Ben down on the gurney. He was limp and still, a nasty bump on his forehead, and unconscious—or worse. The paramedics elbowed Dale out of the way to start work on Ben. Mick squeezed Dale's shoulder, a silent support Dale appreciated.

"Is he all right?" Dale asked as the paramedics examined Ben. He couldn't hold back the panic threading through his words.

"He's alive," the male paramedic said, not taking his eyes off his patient. Dale sagged with relief.

Mick tugged him aside. "Let them do their work."

Dale wanted to argue, but he was needed elsewhere. The fire wasn't fully contained yet. He forced his worry to one side and went back to work.

The fire had spread fiercely through the servants' area, but thanks to the early discovery, it hadn't spread too far through the main part of the house. By the time the fire was out and Dale and the fire crews wearily gathered by the appliances, Ben had been taken to hospital. Dale saw Colson speaking with Tank, although his eyes widened when he saw Joe, the head gardener, with his arm around the butler as if he was never going to let him go.

Tank waved Dale over when he saw him. "They've taken his lordship to hospital as a precaution, but he was conscious when the ambulance left."

Dale breathed easier for the first time since he'd seen Ben lying on the floor. "Thank Christ for that."

"I'm going to the hospital now," Colson said. "I'll call you as soon as I hear anything."

"Tell him I'll be there as soon as I can," Dale said.

"I'll do that." Colson held out his hand to Tank. "Thank you."

"Just doing our job. Thankfully it didn't spread too far."

"His lordship was in the process of installing a sprinkler system in the house. He saw what happened to Clandon Park a couple of years ago. The contractors hadn't finished the work."

"I wonder if someone knew that," Dale said.

Tank frowned. "You think Miller did this? It's a big leap from garden sheds to Calminster Hall."

Dale shrugged. "He had an issue with his lordship. I caught him sounding off in this very spot. The police should talk to his mate—Chris or something like that."

"Chaz Bishop," Tank said.

"Your investigation team can deal with Barry Chalmers, the estate manager," Mr. Colson said, pointing out the estate manager talking to a police officer.

"I must go. His lordship's expecting me."

Dale watched him leave, wishing he could go with him. It was the first time his job had become personal, and he didn't like the feeling.

Tank squeezed his shoulder. "Come on, let's get back to the station. If it's quiet, you can finish the shift early."

Dale smiled gratefully. "Thanks, Tank."

He helped stow away the hoses and climbed into Bertha's cab. As he waited for the rest of the crew, he remembered how he'd thought working in a rural location would be quiet. "I got that wrong," he murmured.

"Got what wrong?" Mick asked as he sat down.

"I thought it would be quiet here. Boring. I've worked harder here than in Nottingham."

"You city boys have it easy."

"I think you're right," Dale agreed.

As they drove back to the station, he shuddered at the thought of how close he'd come to losing Ben. Mick squeezed Dale's shoulder. "Are you okay?"

"Just thinking…."

"Don't," Mick advised. "We found him. That's all that matters."

"What if we hadn't? What was he doing in that room?"

"You'll drive yourself nuts thinking like that," Tank said. "Being in there probably saved him."

Dale knew they were right, but he couldn't let it go. Ben had been minutes away from death, and no one would have found him until it was too late. Dale shuddered at the thought of losing Ben.

Mick patted him, clumsily trying to reassure him. "He'll be fine, Dale. You'll see."

"Okay." Dale nodded, more to reassure Mick than himself. "I know he'll be okay."

AT the station, Lee Fang joined them. "Maloney, Roberts is covering the rest of your shift. Get yourself to the hospital."

Dale smiled at him gratefully. "Thanks, sir. Tell her I'll cover one of hers."

"I will. Get going." Whatever hang-ups Fang had had about Dale and Ben's relationship, he was obviously over it.

"Have you heard from the hospital?"

Fang shook his head. "Give them a chance, Maloney."

Dale thanked him again and headed for his locker. He stripped off his uniform and changed into an old fireman's T-shirt and tracksuit bottoms. He knew he stunk of smoke, but a shower would have to wait until later. Ben was more important.

DALE cursed loudly as he drove to the hospital at a snail's pace, attracting every tractor and slow driver in the county.

"What the hell! Go to fucking Specsavers!" Dale slammed his hand on the steering wheel and screeched at the unhearing driver who pulled out in front of him. "I know I'm in a Mini. I should've fucking driven Bertha. Then you might see me."

By the time he reached A&E, Dale had lost the will to live. Unfamiliar with the hospital layout, Dale drove around twice before he found a parking space. In A&E reception, which was remarkably empty, Dale headed to the desk. The receptionist wrinkled her nose, and Dale realized he probably looked a mess as well as stinking of the fire.

"Yes? May I help you?" she asked.

"Lord Calminster? He came in a short while ago."

"And you are?"

"The fireman who saved his life, and I'm also his partner." Dale leaned forward, and she instinctively took a step back. He had just enough control to leave the *Give me any grief and I'll tear your throat out* unsaid.

"I'll find out for you," she said hastily.

Dale managed a tight smile. "Thank you."

She was back in a couple of minutes. "The doctors are examining him now. If you take a seat, someone will get you when they've finished."

Dale wanted to protest, but he didn't want to get thrown out. He sat down on one of the plastic chairs and waited.

And waited.

And waited.

After half an hour, he went up to the desk again. The receptionist pasted on a smile as Dale approached and asked what was going on.

"I'm sorry, the doctors are still with Lord Calminster."

Dale clenched his hands so tightly, his nails dug into the palms of his hands. "Is he all right? What aren't you telling me?"

"You'll have to wait until they've finished."

After an hour, Dale was at screaming point when the door opened and Colson beckoned him.

"Sorry to keep you waiting. I didn't know you were here," Colson said, exhaustion carving deeper lines around his eyes.

Dale scowled at the receptionist, but she paid no attention to him. "I arrived an hour ago. How is he? The receptionist said the doctors were with him a long time."

"Concussion and smoke inhalation, plus a sprained wrist. They're worried about what he could've inhaled, bearing in mind he was in a cupboard full of chemicals. Come on through."

"Is Ben awake?"

Colson shook his head. "He's asleep at the moment. He had trouble breathing for a while, so they sedated him."

Dale stopped in his tracks. "How bad is he?" he demanded.

"He's breathing on his own. They haven't had to ventilate him. You can sit with him for a while."

Christ! Dale's stomach churned. He'd been a fireman long enough to know what smoke and chemicals did to the lungs. Colson led the way into a room, empty apart from one patient. Dale stopped in the doorway, struggling to breathe himself as he saw Ben, lying still in the bed. Ben was okay. Dale had to keep telling himself that. Aside from the oxygen through a nasal cannula, he was fine.

Colson turned and saw Dale in the throes of his meltdown. He strode over to put his arm around Dale's shoulders. "Mr. Ben is all right, Dale. He's here."

"I know, I'm just being stupid. Just ignore me." Dale sucked in a breath and told himself to man the fuck up. Ben wasn't dead or burned. He just needed time to recover.

"He'll be pleased you're here."

"I should have come with him."

"You had a job to do," Colson said.

Dale pulled a seat close to the bed and sat down, taking Ben's uninjured hand in his. Ben didn't react at all. Dale studied Ben's face, deathly pale through the dirt tracks from the fire.

Colson rubbed his face. "I'll get coffee."

Dale frowned as he tore his eyes away from Ben to look at the butler. "Have you been checked over?"

The man was wrecked.

"I'm fine."

"That's a no, then."

Colson scowled at him. "I wasn't the one trapped in the fire."

"You need to be checked out," Dale insisted.

"I need coffee more."

"Go and get the damn coffee, then get yourself checked by the doctors. I mean it," Dale said sternly as Colson opened his mouth to argue. "Where's Joe?"

Suspicion was written all over Colson's face. "Why?"

"He had his arm around you back at the Hall," Dale pointed out. "I'm sure he wasn't going to let you go anytime soon."

"Someone had to stay and manage the staff. Barry's dealing with the police and fire officers. Joe's going to take care of the staff."

"Mrs. Wilson?" Dale felt guilty. He hadn't given her a second thought in his concern for Ben.

"She's fine. A bit shocked, but she was the one who raised the alarm." Colson shuffled to the door. "Er…. Dale?"

Dale had gone back to staring at Ben again. "Yes?"

"Me and Joe… we…." Colson stared anywhere but at Dale.

"Not my business," Dale said.

"Did Mr. Ben tell you?"

Dale tried not to smirk as Colson asked the question. He looked like he was being dragged across hot coals. "Not a word. But if you were keeping it a secret, I'd say the cat's out of the bag."

"Joe's going to be furious."

"He was the one hugging you in front of everyone," Dale pointed out, and then he did smirk as Colson brightened up.

"So he did!"

Colson went out of the room, almost smiling, and Dale turned his attention back to Ben. He brushed his lips against the back of Ben's hand and grimaced at the acrid taste of fire.

"I'm not going to lose you," Dale murmured, swallowing hard, the lump in his throat making it difficult to breathe. "You're mine, Benedict Raleigh. I love you."

He was sure Ben smiled.

Chapter Eighteen

BEN opened his eyes, blinking sleepily against the sudden light. Something was wrong, but he was too disorientated to work out what it was. He wasn't at the Hall, and this wasn't his bed. Dale was there reading a newspaper. Why was Dale sitting in a chair by his bed?

"Hey, you're awake." Dale grinned at him, a relieved expression in his huge eyes.

"Where…?" Ben removed the mask and tried to moisten his dry mouth. "What happened?"

"Do you remember anything?"

Ben parsed through his memories. "I was…." He wrinkled his brow. "Dogs? Was I walking the dogs? I don't remember."

"There was a fire in the boot room. We found you in the storage room and got you out just in time. Whoa!" Dale pushed Ben back against the pillow as he tried to sit up. "Stay put, okay? You're not hurt, but you breathed in a lot of smoke, and they just want to keep an eye on you."

"Why was I in the storage room?"

"I don't know. Don't you remember going in there?"

"No." Ben wrinkled his brow. "I don't remember."

Dale kissed Ben on the forehead. "Don't worry. It'll come to you."

"The staff? Colson? Are they all right?"

Dale smiled at him as if he was ridiculously pleased about something. "They're fine. They all got out. You were the only one who needed treatment."

"And the Hall?"

"There's damage to the servants' quarters, but—"

Ben sat up, throwing off Dale's restraining hand. He couldn't be lying around in bed all day when his home had been destroyed. "Where are my clothes?"

"What the hell do you think you're doing?" Dale sounded exasperated.

"I'm fine." Ben stood, swaying at the sudden rush to his head.

His moment of being vertical lasted about five seconds, and then he was back on the bed again. He coughed, the action hurting his throat and lungs, but he couldn't stop.

Dale looked unrepentant at virtually throwing Ben back on the bed. He made Ben take a few deep breaths of oxygen, which eased the burning in his lungs. "You're staying put, mate. You breathed in smoke, and until you get the all clear from the docs, you're not going anywhere."

"But—"

"I mean it," Dale growled. "Much as I like seeing your bare arse, you're not well enough to leave."

Bare arse? Ben had no clue what Dale was talking about until he glanced down and realized he was wearing a hospital gown—one of those vile garments that left his back and assets flapping in the breeze.

"I need to get back home," Ben insisted, taking the mask off again. "Is there anything left?"

Dale sighed, confirming Ben's worst fears. Then he sat on the bed and took one of Ben's hands. "The kitchen is destroyed, but the main house is nearly intact."

Ben swallowed hard and blinked away the tears that gathered, not wanting to break down in front of Dale. "How did it start? Was it arson?"

Dale shook his head. "It's too soon to tell. We've got to wait for the place to cool down before our investigators go in. You'll have to find somewhere else to live while the power is off. Your staff, who are amazing, are handling everything."

"Okay." Did anyone need him? Ben took a deep breath, which hurt like hell all the way down his lungs. "I need to be there."

"You need to stay put," Dale said. "Everyone is *fine*, Ben, okay? You're the only one who was hurt."

"Oh." Ben knuckled at his eyes and wished he hadn't, as they stung fiercely. "I'll have to check into a hotel if the power is off."

Carefully, as though he didn't want to frighten a skittish animal, Dale brushed the back of Ben's hand with his lips. "Come stay with me for a few days."

"I don't want to bother you," Ben said.

"Don't be daft. You're welcome to stay."

Ben breathed a sigh of relief at not having to worry for a while until a thought occurred to him. "What will the village say?"

"Who cares?" Dale snapped. "Let the gossips talk. They all know about us. Most of them are just worried about you."

"I need to go home first."

Dale nodded. "When you're released."

Ben yawned, but he was determined to stay awake. "When are the doctors going to spring me?"

As if on cue, a woman walked in the room, an older woman dressed in scrubs whom Ben knew very well.

"Evening, Lord Calminster. Glad to see you're awake." She scowled at Dale. "It would have been useful to know."

"It's been five minutes," Dale protested.

"Leave him alone, Margie," Ben said wearily.

"That's Doctor Margie to you," she said. "I brought you into the world, remember?"

Out of the corner of his eye, Ben could see the surprise on Dale's face. "Dale, meet Dr. Margaret Holmes. She's my family doctor. So, *Doctor* Margie, are you going to let me go?"

"Don't jump fences, young man. You've inhaled lord knows what, and your condition could deteriorate. We want to keep an eye on you overnight."

"But I need to get back home," Ben protested, but Doctor Margie refused to have any of it. Even arguing sapped the little strength Ben possessed. He lay back on thin pillows and yawned.

"Just rest. We'll see you get home as soon as possible." She frowned at Dale. "It's time you went home. You've had a busy day today. Did you tell him what you did?"

Ben was so desperate for them to leave, he almost missed what Doctor Margie said. "What did you say?"

"You mean he didn't tell you?" Margie grinned at them both. "Your fireman is the one who rescued you."

Ben stared at her and then turned to Dale. "Really?"

Dale reddened, obviously embarrassed. "It's my job."

"You saved my life?"

"I got you out of the Hall," Dale said.

Margie snorted. "He threw you over his shoulder."

Ben was gutted. He'd been rescued by a fireman—his fantasy for his entire life—and he'd been unconscious throughout the whole thing. "I don't remember it at all."

"Never mind, Lord Calminster," Margie said. "I'm sure he'd do a reenactment if you ask nicely."

Ben squinted at her sourly. "Haven't you got someone else to annoy?"

Dale smirked at him. "I'm sure I can be persuaded to throw you over my shoulder when you're well enough."

With his doctor in the room—she'd slapped his arse when he was born, for heaven's sake—Ben refused to catch Dale's gaze. Margie's smirk was bigger than Dale's, but Ben ignored them both. He yawned, but that sent shooting pains down his throat.

Margie frowned and spent the next few minutes examining him. Ben made a token protest about all the fuss and attention, but he was too tired to care.

Dale stayed by his side as Margie checked him over, his fingers resting lightly on Ben's arm. He closed his lids just for a moment, because keeping his eyes open was too much like hard work.

BEN heard voices, and Dale speaking, but waking up enough to open his eyes was a struggle. He yawned a couple of times and blinked.

"He's stirring." Mrs. Wilson patted his hand. "Hello, Mr. Ben. Good to see you awake."

"Did you start the party without me?" he rasped. Ben took a while to get out the sentence, his throat was so raw.

Dale pushed the hair back from Ben's face. "Are you all right?"

"Yes. No. Ask me later." Ben had no clue just how he felt.

"It's okay."

Ben started to cough.

Dale slipped his arm around Ben and supported him. Pain racked Ben's chest, and he was relieved when he finally stopped enough to drawn in another breath. Dale eased Ben onto the pillow and then stood back as a nurse came into the room.

"I think his lordship needs to rest," she said.

Mrs. Wilson nodded, and Colson helped her to her feet. "We'll be back tomorrow."

"I'm going to be home tomorrow," Ben insisted; then he coughed again.

The nurse made a humming noise as she checked his pulse and blood pressure. "I'm just going to get the doctor to examine you. I'll be back in a moment."

"Is everything all right?" Dale asked.

"His stats have dropped a little. Not a lot, but we need to keep a close eye on him."

Ben knocked the mask off. "Is it serious?"

Dale put the mask back in place. "It's just precautionary." Ben frowned at him, but Dale just sat down and took his hand. "Why don't you go to have a nap for a while?"

"Why don't you go home?" Ben suggested.

"I'm not leaving you."

"But—"

Dale shook his head. "I'm staying here until they throw me out. Close your eyes and nap. I'll play on my phone for a while."

Ben thought about arguing, but he was exhausted, and a brief nap seemed like a really good idea. He yawned, grimacing as his throat and lungs registered their protest.

Dale stroked Ben's hair again. "I'm so glad I found you. I don't know what I would've done if—"

"Don't even think about it," Ben said sleepily.

"I can't help it."

Ben fumbled until he found Dale's face and cupped his jaw. "I'm fine. I told you you're a hero. You're my hero."

Dale kissed Ben's forehead. "Sleep now. I won't leave you alone."

Chapter Nineteen

ALTHOUGH Dale was still new to the station, Fang allowed him to take a few days leave while Ben was in hospital. Dale stayed by Ben's side until he was thrown out at night—like a fucking guard dog, Ben muttered constantly. Dale ignored his complaints. He noticed Ben's language was less Lord Calminster these days, and more like the firefighters' mess. Ben tried to plaster an aristocratic sneer on his face when Dale pointed this out, but it descended into giggles when Dale tickled him. Ben was very ticklish.

Ben kept a polite smile on his face for the constant stream of visitors to his room, only breathing a sigh of relief when they left. He only dropped the mask for Dale, Colson, and Mrs. Wilson. The latter brought food and insisted Dale took breaks while she was there to mind his lordship. Ben, Colson, and Dale did as they were told because, after all, it was Mrs. Wilson.

The smile on Ben's face was somewhat strained after forty-eight hours of being poked, prodded, and x-rayed. By the time he was officially discharged, Ben was barely speaking to anyone, including Dale. Dale didn't know what to say or do to make him feel better. The situation hadn't improved when Lee Fang confirmed they were treating the fire as arson, and Olly Miller was their prime suspect.

Once Ben discovered the power had been restored safely to the Hall, he decided to go home rather than staying at Dale's cottage. Dale was disappointed about Ben's decision, but as Ben had retreated into sullen silence, perhaps it was for the best. He drove up the long driveway to Calminster Hall, deciding to deliver Ben into the care of Mr. Colson and leave him alone. However, as Dale parked, he caught sight of Ben's white face as he stared up the blackened side of the outer building near the kitchen.

Dale ran around the car and put his arm around Ben's shoulders. "It's okay, Ben. I know it looks bad, but the kitchen took the brunt of the fire. The upstairs and the rest of the house is barely touched."

"My home," Ben whispered.

Dale turned Ben into his chest and stroked his hair. After a few days, Ben's thick curls were greasy, and Dale wanted to get him inside and clean him up. "I promise you we can fix this."

Ben snorted. "Like you did the pole?"

"It might take more than a few firefighters and a tin of paint," Dale admitted. "But it can be fixed. Come on, let's get you settled."

He coaxed Ben up the steps. Colson opened the door, and the dogs rushed out to greet Ben, Fluffy throwing himself at his master in his eagerness to attract his attention. Dale stood back to give Ben some space as he knelt down to love his animals.

"They've been so depressed without Mr. Ben."

Dale smiled at Mrs. Wilson, who had joined him. "I didn't even think about the dogs," he admitted.

"You had more important things to think about," she said. "Besides, there were enough of us here to look after the mutts."

The dogs momentarily calmed, Ben turned to Mrs. Wilson and took her hands. "I'm sorry, Mrs. Wilson."

She furrowed her brow. Dale was puzzled too, not sure what Ben was apologizing for.

"I had no idea what it was like to lose your home. I've been feeling sorry for myself the last couple of days. But you lost everything."

Her chin wobbled, but Mrs. Wilson nodded as she held on to his hands. "The fire in my cottage was partly my fault. Sandra was always scolding me for having tea towels so close to the cooker. Your beautiful home has been destroyed because a foolish man had a grudge against you."

Dale growled because if he ever got his hands on Miller, he was going to string him up by the nutsac and leave him there for a piñata. He didn't say it out loud because he didn't want to offend Mrs. Wilson. Ben obviously heard the growl, because he rolled his eyes at Dale.

"If I ever get my hands on that man, I'm chopping him up for dog meat," Mrs. Wilson declared.

Dale smiled in satisfaction. Perhaps he should voice his thoughts in the future. He had a feeling Mrs. Wilson wasn't easily offended.

Ben's eyes were going to roll out of his sockets. "I'm surrounded by savages."

Colson coughed politely. "Why don't you sit down, and I'll bring afternoon tea. We've set up a temporary kitchen in the dining room."

Fresh snow had more color than Ben's face and Dale was sure he was holding himself together by sheer will as he said, "Show me the kitchen first."

Dale guided Ben down the stairs. Ben's face grew tighter as he saw the blackened walls and ceiling. The kitchen was a mess, the furniture that was left just amorphous black blobs.

"The structure is still sound," Dale said. "It won't take long to repair."

"Show me the rest," Ben ordered.

Colson took him around the rest of the servants' quarters until he'd seen the devastation for himself. Ben's face grew tighter and whiter until Dale got toppy and insisted Ben sat down.

"Afternoon tea now, please, Mr. Colson," Dale said. He ignored Ben's protests and steered him to his private study. The hall reeked of smoke, but there was no obvious damage. Ben stumbled once but Dale was there to hold him, and he collapsed as soon his legs touched the back of the sofa.

"I don't need another cup of bloody tea." Ben had complained long and loud about how much tea they were forcing down his throat in hospital.

As usual, Dale ignored the complaints. "Sit, relax, drink tea, and then I'll give you the guided tour."

"This is my damned house. I want to see it now."

"Fucking sit there before I tie you down," Dale snapped. "They're all trying to keep it together for you."

Ben subsided with a pout. "I know that."

Dale took a deep breath and made an effort to soften his tone. "Let them pamper you for today. Mrs. Wilson is one flap away from a meltdown, and Colson doesn't know whether to hug you, shackle you to the bed, or run to Joe's hut and never come out."

Ben opened his mouth and then closed it again. "You know about Colson and Joe?"

"Joe had his arms around Colson."

"In public?" Ben smirked at Dale.

"Yep, but I'm under orders not to mention it to your burly gardener."

"Burly gardener?" Ben burst out laughing. "I've got a hot butler and a burly gardener? Sounds like a porn movie."

"I wouldn't mind watching those two together." Dale waggled his eyebrows suggestively.

Ben smacked him on the bicep. "You're disgusting."

"You can't tell me you don't think the same thing."

"Dale, they're my butler and gardener."

"Porn, man, I'm telling you."

Ben made a gagging noise, which turned into choking as Colson walked into the room with a tray. Dale snickered and sat on one of the armchairs. He knew Ben was totally grossed out by the thought, but he watched Colson pour the tea. Damn, the man had a fine arse. He was totally aware of Ben's glare as Colson left the room.

"I'm going to kill you," Ben said.

"Sure you are."

"I am."

"Aw, then I won't be able to do my reenactment of rescuing you," Dale said.

Ben raised his eyebrow. "You're going to throw me over your shoulder again?"

"I thought being rescued by a fireman was your fantasy?"

"Hell, yes. Only in my fantasy, I was awake to remember it."

"Then I'll rescue you again." Dale mimed throwing someone over his shoulder.

Ben sighed and leaned back against the sofa, and the energy seeped out of him. "Maybe not today."

"I can wait." Dale moved to the sofa and took Ben into his arms. "Go to sleep for a while. There's nothing for us to do."

Ben sighed and relaxed in Dale's arms. "I'm supposed to be the master of the house."

"You are, but I'm the master of you. 'Kay?"

Ben pressed a kiss into Dale's chest. "'Kay."

Dale held him close until Ben's breathing slowed. He grinned when he heard a snorting, snoring noise. Dale wriggled a bit as his arse went numb. He was going to have to persuade Ben to get a more comfortable sofa in his private study. Maybe something made this century.

He was almost dozing himself when his phone rang. Dale fumbled to get it quickly before it disturbed Ben, only to cut off the call. Dale cursed under his breath. He went to return the call; then it rang again.

"Dale?"

Dale frowned. His station commander was the last person he expected to hear from. "Sir? Is everything okay?"

"I need to speak to his lordship. I can't get hold of him. Do you know where he is?"

"He's asleep. Can it wait?"

"Not really. Miller's on his way over to you. He ran away from a fire near the café. They chased him into the trees, but he gave the slip."

"Fuck!"

"PC Verne's on his way over," Fang said. "And Tank and the crew are coming in Buffy."

"I'll alert the security guards and the rest of the staff." Dale stood, trying to keep the phone tucked under his ear and settle Ben on the sofa without waking him. "Thanks for calling."

"Keep in touch."

Dale made sure Ben was still asleep and then checked the windows. He briefly contemplated locking Ben in, but the thought of Ben not being able to escape in the event of another fire made his blood run cold.

The first person he told was Colson. The butler's face tightened, but he immediately got on the phone to security. Then he phoned Joe.

Dale waited until he finished. "Lord Calminster is asleep in his study. I want to talk to my crew, who are on their way."

Colson nodded. "I'll make sure the house is locked down. Then I'll stay with him."

Dale left him and went to the dining room. Mrs. Wilson and Lisa smiled at him when he entered, but their smiles soon faded when he told them about Miller.

"He'd better not come in here," Mrs. Wilson growled, brandishing a large chopping knife.

"Don't take any risks," Dale said. "I'll make sure my boys look after you."

She pointed the knife. "We're not helpless, dear."

Dale had no doubt of that. "Make sure the windows are locked."

"I'll do that." Lisa hopped up and went over to the windows.

"Er.... Dale. There's a man running towards the house and a load of hunky firemen running after him." She squinted. "I think some of them are your lot."

Dale rushed over to the window to join her. "Hunky firemen? Where?"

She laughed as Dale groaned. "You need your eyes checked, Lisa. Tank and Mick are not hunky."

"Got you over here, though."

Dale snorted. "I ought to check all the windows are closed along this wing."

"Do you think he's going to make the house? Have you seen how fast your guys are going?"

It was almost comical. Miller pounded toward the house, but hard on his heels were Verne, Tank, Keith, and Mick. They were within arms' length when suddenly Miller was tackled from the side.

"What the hell?" Dale said.

"Joe's taken him down." Lisa punched the air. "Go Calminster!"

The four firemen stood around Miller while Joe got to his feet. Sensibly, Miller stayed on the ground.

"I think I'll go back to Ben," Dale said.

"You know he's going to be angry you didn't wake him up," Lisa said.

Dale shrugged. "He'll forgive me eventually. I have my ways."

Lisa made a gagging noise. "Ewww, I don't want to think about that."

"Lisa!" Mrs. Wilson scolded. "That's enough of that."

Dale decided to vanish before he got told off.

The door to the study was locked. Dale panicked for a moment until he remembered Colson was with

Ben. He knocked on the door. "It's over. Miller's been caught."

"Hold on," Colson said. He unlocked the door and stepped out, closing the door behind him. "Mr. Ben is still asleep. You said Miller is in custody?"

"Well, now he's crashed out on the lawn," Dale said. "The police and firefighters were almost on him, but he got taken out by a burly gardener."

Colson's lips twitched. "It's porn all over again. Just missing the hot butler!"

Dale's cheeks flushed. "You heard that conversation."

"I have very good hearing," Colson said, not bothering to hide his smirk.

"Oh God."

"I'll go and see if they need help."

"I'll go and hide—forever." Dale waited until Colson had walked down the corridor before he thumped his forehead on the door.

Then, still blushing, Dale opened the door. Ben stirred, blinking sleepily. "Hey, where did you go?"

"Just went to see Mrs. Wilson. Are you okay?"

Ben sat up, yawned loudly, and scratched his belly. "Just tired."

Dale sat down next to him and kissed Ben on the mouth. "You can relax in your own bed tonight."

"I don't think I'm ever going to relax until Miller is caught," Ben admitted.

"In which case you can sleep like a baby."

Ben tried to get up but Dale pulled him back, tugging Ben into his arms. "He's been caught? Where? Why didn't you wake me?"

"You missed the gardener in action."

Ben furrowed his brow, obviously confused. "What?"

Dale placed a finger over Ben's mouth. "I'm going to kiss you."

"But—"

Ben faded off into a moan as Dale kissed him. Ben could be the Lord of Calminster in a few moments. Right this second, he could be Dale's.

Coming in November 2017

DREAMSPUN DESIRES

Dreamspun Desires #45
Game Point by M.J. O'Shea

Game, set… match made in heaven.

Spoiled socialite Quinn Valenzuela has no interest in sports or his family's huge sporting goods empire, Sparta Athletics. So when Quinn learns his grandfather has died and he's in control of the corporation, no one is more surprised than Quinn himself.

Dedicated COO Porter Davis has little time and less patience for brats like Quinn who have never done a day's work, but circumstances leave him with little choice. Quinn claims he's ready to leave partying behind and grow up, but it'll take more than words to earn Porter's respect. As it turns out, they can work—and play—together after all. A friends with benefits arrangement makes sense for the two busy men, but are they too different for it to ever develop into more? Not if Quinn can convince Porter he has his head in the game.

Dreamspun Desires #46
The Secret of the Sheikh's Betrothed by Felicitas Ivey

Billionaire Fathi al-Murzim is a workaholic businessman, too busy running the family's various companies to even think about marriage. Too bad he never told his grandfather he's gay, because he's just announced a childhood betrothal—to a Bedouin girl Fathi never heard about before.

Ikraam din Abdel was raised as a woman by his avaricious older sister, who didn't want him to be their father's heir. He'd never thought to be married either, and is surprised when his sister informs him of his betrothal.

When they meet, they are drawn to each other in a manner neither of them expected. As the plans for their wedding progress, both of them realize that they need to tell the other the truth. But can they, with both cultural taboos and family pressures to deal with?

Love Always Finds a Way

DREAMSPUN DESIRES
Subscription Service

Love eBooks?

Our monthly subscription service gives you two eBooks per month for one low price. Each month's titles will be automatically delivered to your Dreamspinner Bookshelf on their release dates.

Prefer print?

Receive two paperbacks per month! Both books ship on the 1st of the month, giving you *exclusive* early access! As a bonus, you'll receive both eBooks on their release dates!

Visit
www.dreamspinnerpress.com
for more info or to sign up now!

FOR **MORE** OF THE **BEST GAY ROMANCE**

DREAMSPINNER PRESS
dreamspinnerpress.com

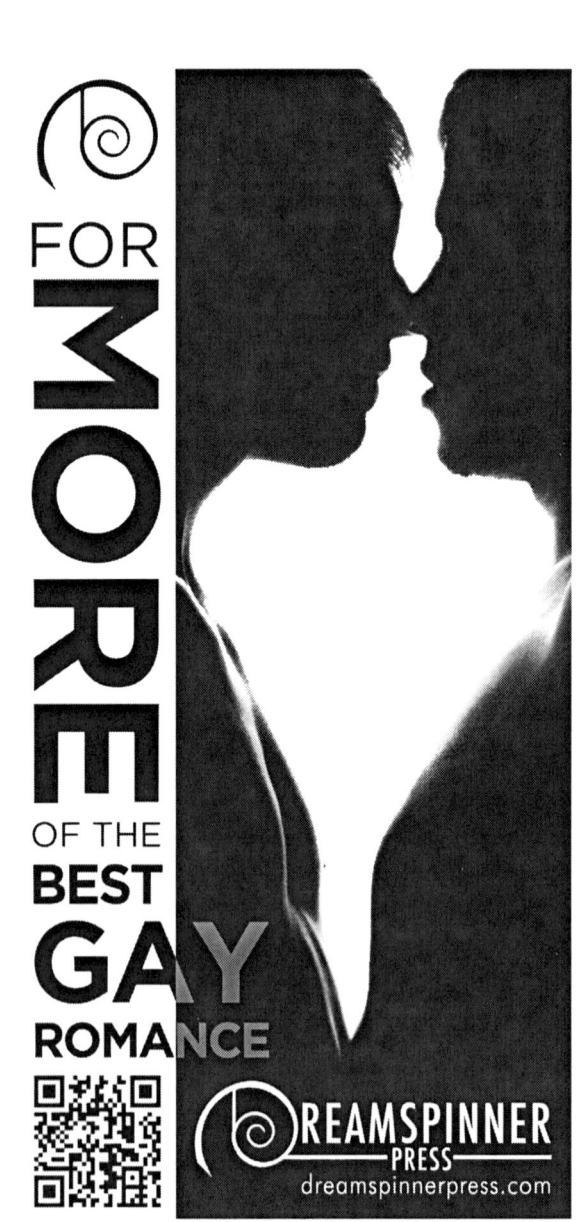

CPSIA information can be obtained
at www.ICGtesting.com
Printed in the USA
LVOW12s1432130318
569702LV00001B/9/P